TRIBAL GODS

MAEVE CASEY

WORDSONTHESTREET

First published in 2018
by
Wordsonthestreet
Six San Antonio Park, Salthill, Galway, Ireland

www.wordsonthestreet.com
publisher@wordsonthestreet.com
@wordsstreet

ISBN 978-1-907017-45-2

Cover design, layout and typesetting: Wordsonthestreet

TRIBAL GODS

ABOUT THE AUTHOR

Maeve Casey grew up in Limerick, worked with Aer Lingus and travelled widely. She then qualified as a psychologist and worked at the Social Psychology Research Unit and the Women's Studies Centre at University College Dublin. Her short stories have been published in New Irish Writing and broadcast on RTÉ Radio 1 and on BBC Radio 4. She now lives with her husband in Dublin where *Tribal Gods*, her first novel, is set.

As always, for Jim —
more than words can say.

ACKNOWLEDGEMENTS

In researching this novel I am indebted to the works of the mythologist Joseph Campbell, particularly his text *The Hero with a Thousand Faces* (New York: Paladin, 1988). I was particularly influenced by his narrations on the hero as redeemer, the hero as warrior, and the somewhat neglected hero as lover. Sincere thanks too to Robin Morgan for her brilliantly insightful work on the Greek heroic quest — *The Demon Lover on the Sexuality of Terrorism* (New York: Norton, 2001) — so influential in Irish literature at the time of the first Celtic revival. For those eager for further analysis on this topic my own academic papers *On Bloods: Of Wombs and Tombs — Blood Mysteries and Blood Sacrifice* (Trinity College Dublin, Mercy Not Sacrifice Conference, 2007) and *Paradoxical Reconciliation as a New Horizon* (EFECIS Conference, Seville University, 2007) may also be of interest.

1

You died and I didn't know.

At one forty-two, yesterday, Wednesday. Where was I just then, that moment as you breathed your last? I'd had lunch, yes, an apple and cheese, had left for a brisk walk along the seafront, part of the 'move more, eat less' regime you'd endlessly advocated for me. Does it matter much now that I might lose half a stone, now, in the face of this?

Drove the car to Sandycove harbour to walk from there. Were you still alive as I parked on that, just another day, pleased to have found a space, smugly pleased too to have found one free of double-yellow lines. How could such trivia have mattered so and how distant that all seems now.

I weaved my way through the tourists that streamed towards Joyce's tower; did you still breathe then? The tide was out, yes I remember that; the news of your death might have obliterated all recall, but no, the large rocks were seaweed-draped and beyond them the sea a glassy blue. I waved to Joe Lydon as he threw stones for his dogs, heard their loud splash, then saw a nearby heron spread its wide wings and soar. Farther down the promenade visitors queued at Teddy's for ices, how many times as schoolgirls had we queued together there? Walked past the remains of the Victorian bathhouse – remember glancing at my watch with satisfaction then, and assured I walked briskly, for strolling is useless for losing weight. Yet the first of the summer strawberries for sale at the top of the pier tempted with their promise of thick, fresh cream.

You were still alive as I approached the bandstand, for I recall glancing at my watch again then, just then, one ten, so I'd time to walk to the lighthouse and back, as you battled to live on. That's what I can't stand, the fact that you died alone. We, who used to giggle together in girlish terror at tales of death knocks and ghosts, why did neither bother to haunt me just then at all? A band played at the Victorian stand, Verdi's *Chorus of the Hebrew Slaves* – *(Speed Your Journey)*. Might I have sensed your passing from that?

The harbour to my left was filled with small boats as I passed it, and the children within them circled and sailed as I climbed down the narrow steps to the lower pier to view them. Most wore bright orange life jackets, a few yellow tops, as they fought to steer and remain afloat. Two boats overturned and the youngsters floundered in the water, but not for long, while three were carried out beyond the lighthouses towards the open sea. I watched as the two larger boats that followed corralled them back inside.

I walked on swiftly again, paused briefly at the plaque to Beckett, stood on the spot where the great genius claimed that all, all had at last been revealed to him there. Well, good for our Sam, our Mr B. No mystery left?

A nurse found you dead, one for whom I expect that final rite of passage is as commonplace as this summer walk is for me.

'Ms Leahy, please.'

'Speaking.'

'Close friend of Grace Donovan's, I believe.'

'Yes, we've known each other from childhood.'

'Sad news, I'm afraid. She's died.'

Silence

'Hello? ... Hello? You still there?'

'Yes. I believed she'd recover. Thank you. Thank you for calling.'

'Only child. Single. Parents deceased. No next of kin. Could you inform those close to her, the people to whom she mattered, before you hit the papers?'

'Yes. Yes. I'll see what I can do.'

I'd so believed you'd get well, and if my field of science had nothing further to offer I'd even have pleaded with the god I no longer believe in for your survival. Had conned myself into believing that you would definitely do so. But inform those who were close to you? However can I do that?

Juan? How could I get to tell him? Where is he now? With a plump Spanish wife and a hoard of olive-skinned kids? You loved him once, when he was just nineteen. You even boasted triumphantly to my still-maidenly self that you'd lost your virginity to him wearing only your pearls, just like Dotty in *The Group*. Did his Mediterranean soul, unlike mine, sense your passing, recall you suddenly, unexpectedly, as you left life, and unlike me, somehow know?

You'd a priest lover too. Why wasn't he with you at the end, when Catholics do death so well? All those secretive years he played Abelard to your Heloise and he not with you either. He may even still fumble furtively beneath his celibate sheets to your memory – God forgive him, for I never will. Do you still live on as some erotic holy spirit in his tortured soul? I can't contact him, how could I when his demands for secrecy were such that you refused to even tell me his name, when I knew him only as your Father Y.

Yes, I will phone Brendan. Shocking to have him learn of your death in tomorrow's paper, couldn't be so cruel as to allow that. Know him from work anyway; he consultant to my pharmacist, how different he was in his treatment of patients as opposed to staff. 'And how are we today, Mrs Connors?' Fangs cheesily bared, the control freak you loved. Tamed you, I fear, at least for a time, when all prior to him had failed. I will phone him tonight, hope his wife doesn't answer, that's all. Your flamboyant self's replacement, Ms Prissy Prim. No, better phone his office; maybe even upset one of his megabucks medical deals. Or I could allow him read it in the newspaper, be as uncaring as he was to you. No, I wouldn't do that.

I will chase up Andy too, he's still in New Zealand, has a brother in the city somewhere who'll have a contact phone number, I expect. Went there, it was rumoured on the city grapevine, to escape your clutches, to nurse his broken heart, perhaps even both. I know he offered to marry you, you once told me that. Marriage … he respected the institution, felt he'd paid you the ultimate compliment, but you were determined to remain free to follow your heart right 'til the end.

And Paul, less difficult to contact him, though he may well be abroad on business or at some race meeting. The married Paul, last of your five loves. You were thirty-four by then and didn't much care how some labelled you as his 'bit on the side'. Had a wife when you met, but triangles gave you a buzz, added a spice that you richly savoured. I recall that night you first met. Your fingers curled around a brandy glass, fingernails long and red as those that peeped out from the toe of your high-heeled sandal. The third nail on your right hand was chipped; that imperfection irritated you for you glanced at it several times then attempted to cover it with your left hand. I doubt if he noticed, or, if he had, that it would have mattered much to him. I saw his gaze scan the guests then halt at you. Pause again at your

Carmen lips, at the hint of cleavage by your neckline, then down past the flow of your red dress to your tanned legs.

You gazed back at him, some might say brazenly, and then the mysterious moment you so yearned for happened, his gaze met yours, locked and held, and, in the midst of that crowded, noisy party, all others faded; only you two were there. I saw you nod, and then he nodded too, heard you excuse yourself and leave, and then watched as he followed you outside.

How long ago all that seems now, but then we, Grace, my soul sister, we first became friends, even further back. Until ... no, I'll not think of that ... that violence ... not now ... for what happened then changed me, changed you too. And, yet again, around that fear that seems to underpin all fears, yes, that same one, the fear of death.

'You're crying. What's wrong?'

Rose Leahy continued to weep softly as she looked up from the church pew and saw Grace Donovan. She didn't know her well, for although they both wore the same school uniform, the grey gymslip, cream blouse and grey and yellow striped tie of Saint Martha's, Grace was in sixth class, and a year ahead of her. Rose knew her as daring, some said even brazen, one who had been named publicly at assembly for wearing her hats thrown to the back of her head and secured with a hat pin (chin band invisible), her black hair flowing loose behind it rather than secured neatly, all strictly forbidden.

'I'm dying.' Rose's voice came as a quiet sob in the empty church.

Grace looked at her curiously, noting the young girl's blotched cheeks and swollen eyes, yet she seemed healthy otherwise. 'Why d'you think that?' she asked, noting too, and with some disapproval, that her nails were bitten down to the quick, while the mandatory hat elastic, which Grace hated, made a black crease around her white neck.

'Because of the blood,' she whispered. 'I've tried to stop it and I've prayed and prayed, but it still keeps coming.'

'Where? I can't see any.'

'Between my legs. I saw it at three, and now there's more, I can feel it. I don't want to die, I don't …'

'Did your mam not tell you? That's just your first period. Mine came a year ago.' Rose glanced up furtively and wished she didn't speak so loud. 'And look, I'm still alive. It just means you're growing up. Look,' she followed Rose's gaze then lowered her voice, 'boys would die if they bled for five days, but we don't. We,' she claimed with a grand air of triumph, 'bleed for five days each month and live.'

Rose remained unsure. Beyond Grace she observed an empty church save for the effigies to saints that peopled its side walls and with whom she'd pleaded and prayed that she might live. First to Saint Anthony, his shrine to her right. True, he'd been dead for hundreds of years, yet her grandmother still wrote SAG on every envelope she addressed to ensure its safe arrival. To Saint Francis, who was dead too and to whom Mr Phelan wheeled his son each Saturday and prayed for a miracle, as the doctors had said they could do nothing more for him. And after she'd gone to the loo and looked again for the third time and the blood was still there, she'd finally turned to Saint Jude, the saint for hopeless cases. Yet, all about her, only the flowers that crowded the Virgin's shrine and Grace seemed to live, for the white roses bloomed large as they mixed with lush greenery while several Easter lilies with yellow centres rose between them. 'How did you know,' she asked her new-found friend curiously, 'that I was here?'

'I didn't,' Grace replied, 'just came early to practise for the choir. I sing solo with them at rosary and benediction.' She glanced at her watch. 'It starts in about ten minutes.' Rose watched her leave and walk up the aisle. 'Stay and listen if you want,' she called over her shoulder, 'and after – it's nothing to fear – stay on and I'll walk home with you.' She paused by the piano then turned the pages of the musical score, which made a shuffling sound in the silent church.

Bring flowers of the fairest
Bring blossoms the rarest
From garden and woodland and hillside and vale.

Rose listened, her thighs clutched tightly together, the blood still damp between her legs. 'Did that sound alright to you?' Grace called down to her. 'Can you hear me from there?'

'You could use the mike.'

'You mean you can't hear me?'

'I can, but it'd be easier on your voice.'

'Can't, there's only one mike and Father William always hocks it.'

Our strong hearts are swelling
Our glad voices telling
In praise of the loveliest flower of the vale.

The church began to fill and Rose saw three rows of sixth-formers file in neatly behind Grace, heard the soft ping of the tuning fork and saw Miss Behan give the choir the note, before she went and sat at the piano. She didn't want to stay, yet her hands grew sweaty at the prospect of walking down the church aisle to the curious gaze of the congregation and going home alone. She bowed her head as the rosary began, and heard Father William's loud *Hail Mary, full of Grace* fill the church, followed by the murmured *Holy Mary, mother of God* congregational response. The repetitive decades made her drowsy and she longed to sit up on the pew yet dared not do so as all the others knelt, so she closed her eyes and allowed the rhythmic chant flow towards and all around her. She was startled when it ceased, to the rattle of beads being returned to purses and catches being snapped shut. *Salve Regina, Mater Misericordiae* sang Grace in her strong voice as benediction began, and then the choir sang *Tantum Ergo* and she watched Father William remove the consecrated host from the golden tabernacle. *This is my body, this is my blood.* The heady smell of incense, burning candle wax and spring flowers wafted outwards and beyond him, while the sanctuary lamp flickered its message of eternal presence.

'Have you much homework?' Grace asked, as they wound their way past the blood thorn that bloomed beyond the church wall, and before Rose could answer she confided that her essay on 'My favourite character from history' was due on the morrow, that she hadn't even begun it, but had decided to tell of one historic 'Grace' who shared her name.

'Grace O'Malley?' asked Rose, who didn't like history much, saw little point in a subject where all the characters were well dead.

'Yes, I could write about her,' her new friend agreed, 'and there's plenty to say, how she owned her own fleet of ships, lived in a castle in Mayo, married three times, and how Queen Elizabeth was her friend.'

'But all that's yonks ago,' Rose responded scornfully, then paused as they reached the metals before jumping hopscotch-style from flagstone to flagstone as they crossed. 'Grace Gifford's a better story,' Rose called back as she reached the far side first, 'married at midnight, inside a jail, then six hours later the Brits shoot her husband dead. They were both artists and ...'

'I know, she painted, and I'd love to sing her husband's poem, *I See His Blood Upon the Rose,* but no one's ever put it to music.'

'But they're both dead,' she said, frightened again. 'Why don't you do your essay on Grace Kelly, she may even visit Ireland soon.'

'Yeah, I know she's not history yet, but why should I care about that? I want to grow up just like her, be beautiful and famous and loved by film stars and princes.'

That confidence surprised Rose, who knew Miss Kelly from the film *High Noon* as blonde and tall, while Grace Donovan was dark-haired and sallow-skinned; it had even been hinted more than once that some Armada genes lurked deep within that Donovan girl. 'My mam's so old,' she continued, 'and 'cause she feared she'd never have a child, my surprise arrival was seen as a gift, like divine Grace. But I can't write that, can I? Anyway, why were you called Rose?'

'I don't know, it's just the name of a flower.'

'But if you had to write an essay like mine, what would you say?'

Rose thought for a time. 'I'd tell of the Little Flower, I suppose,' she said at last, 'of Saint Teresa of the Roses ...' she glanced at Grace, and found she listened with eagerness '... and that her convent at Lisieux was near to Flanders, and that the French loved her and the Irish and the Austrians soldiers who fought on opposite sides both prayed to her. But I much prefer maths, and, most of all, I got a chemistry set for Christmas and I'd just love to take science.'

'Only for boys, and you're definitely not that,' Grace laughed. The comment made Rose uncomfortable again and conscious of the damp red blood between her thighs. 'Miss Behan says I'm for the classics,' Grace continued, as Rose struggled to silence her fear, for the head teacher who wore tweed skirts and well-washed cardigans that drained her tired face imparted the classics to those of her brighter students destined for the convent, while her 'duds' were trained in domestic science merely for marriage and family. Grace giggled as they reached the hotel wall, then paused. 'You know the speech that she gives every day at the start of her class? I've heard it so often I know it by heart.' She assumed her teacher's authoritative voice. '"You will join my final class, Rose Leahy, for soon I retire. And there, for one last time I will impart to you, and my better students, the ancient beauty of the Greek mythologies and the Latin language, coupled with the heroic valour of their warrior class."'

'Grace, you're a screech, you sound just like her. When I close my eyes I think it's Behan I hear.'

'"This state's move to science,"' her new friend continued grandly, '"to industrialisation, is now inevitable; we classicists have lost. So what does the future promise this island? A new race, one of mere technocrats. Educate for work, for jobs, for the factory, but what of the terrible price should we bid farewell to the ancient wisdoms of Greece and Rome, where the epic warrior quest, the struggle of boy, of man, and of hero with blood sacrifice is so well told. They may well educate the worker, but who, pray now, will educate the man?'"

'What would she know?' Rose giggled. 'She's only a spinster, an old maid.'

'My mam says she's unclaimed treasure. And I know something else too, it's said that long ago, when she was young, that she was unlucky in love.'

'She failed to get a man, and should have been a nun. Have you got a boy yet? You know, your own boyfriend?'

'No, I just wish I had. I know Jack Ryan from the choir alright, but he's useless now, his voice has broken and he can't sing with me anymore. I miss him, he was our best soprano, and we don't know if his singing voice will ever come back. In the past, you know,' her voice sank to a whisper, 'they'd have sliced off his balls to preserve his beautiful voice for God.'

Rose looked aghast. 'I've to get home,' she said, and moved on hurriedly.

'Wait, we'll just stop at Teddy's, I've money for two ninety-nines. A cone with whipped ice-cream and chocolate, that'll cheer you up.'

Rose ate quickly before the white and brown cone melted and dribbled down their fingers. 'We go to Greystones for July,' she boasted as they hurried on.

Once there, her father fished and occasionally brought her along for company. She secretly found the holiday month boring, but pretended otherwise, remained silent too of her new-found nervousness as she told Grace about the live fish that wriggled on his line and that he triumphantly bashed dead with a stone, later to be served up for dinner.

'I prefer Brittas,' Grace confided, and went on to boast that they spent each August there, told how her father golfed, and then returned from the links to picnic in the sand dunes with his family, and how they all swam afterwards in the salty waves.

As they neared her home Rose grew frightened again, fearful that her mother, angry at her late arrival, just wouldn't listen to her explanations. Was she still bleeding, was there even more blood? Grace, though still mysteriously alive, had confided that she would bleed each month for five whole days! Was that so? The garden pathway cut its way through a neat lawn and tidy flowerbeds that promised an early summer, and, as she rang the doorbell, she glanced back to her new friend, who waved and then moved on. She heard her mother's familiar footsteps approach, the door opened, and she went inside.

When Grace opened her hall door on Sunday night, she found Rose standing outside. 'I bought a gift to thank you,' she said, holding out a parcel shyly.

'Oh, hi. Come in.'

'My mam thought I might buy you a record,' Rose said as she followed her into the kitchen, 'or maybe a book token, even a box of Milk Tray or Black Magic. Anyway, she said I was to buy something you'd really like.'

'Let me see.' Grace tore eagerly at the wrapping. 'Yes,' she cried, 'nothing better.'

'It's close to Grace Kelly's hair colour, I took just forever to decide which dye was best. "Bashful Blonde" wasn't really you, or "Frivolous Fawn" either. I thought "Coy Ash" sounded nice, "Dazzling Gold" looked a bit brash, though they'd three for the price of two on that shade. I decided on "Sunlight Serenade" in the end. Hope you like it.'

'Great. We'll do it now, straight away.'

That suggestion surprised Rose, made her suddenly nervous. 'Where's your mother?' she asked, glancing around.

'My parents? They're at bridge.' Grace assumed a father's voice of weary tolerance. '"Trumped again, Lena, and by Mrs Ryan too. When I led with my Jack, why didn't you follow with your Queen?" That'll just go on and on, as if I don't exist. Come on, we'll go blonde together, right away.'

'It's a present for you, not for me,' Rose protested, though swept along by Grace's delight at her choice of gift as she eagerly lay out the contents of the box on the table. Light gloves in see-through plastic, a measuring thimble, small spoon, and two sachets of white powder. 'Read the instructions,' she commanded.

'They're in German, and French. English here at last. 'First test on a small lock of hair.'

'Don't bother with that, we don't have time. How much water do I add to the powder, that's the main thing, then you comb it through my hair, then I'll do yours, give you a few blonde streaks as well.'

'...wait for twenty minutes then rinse out.'

'Great. Here goes.'

She combed the white newly mixed substance through Grace's black hair, dye that reeked powerfully of ammonia, with fumes that itched her nose, made her sneeze and caused her eyes to water. She felt her scalp tingle as Grace applied it to her head, and grew silently alarmed when she glanced at the clock and realised that they'd failed to time the application accurately. Then they waited — Grace chatting eagerly about her essay, now complete, and her voice training, the classes she took weekly, her secret dream to be a singer — until they finally rinsed their heads and viewed the transformation. Grace's jet-black hair was now a marmalade orange shade, streaked like Mrs Ryan's tabby cat in light and darker shadings, while her own lighter colour boasted several strands that were prematurely white. But Grace swung her hair from side to side with delight, boastful, come Monday, of being the centre of attention with all her classmates.

Rose stood as instructed on the wide school dais and shivered. Below her, a sea of upturned faces, of the assembled fourth, fifth and sixth classes, watched in silence as Miss Behan summoned Grace centre stage. The steel blades of the scissors she held peered out from beneath the darned cuff of her cardigan then narrowed to two sharp points. She swept Grace's hair back from her right ear then placed the cold steel close by her neck. The assembled school watched in hushed silence, no sound save the creak of Miss Behan's rubber soles as she circled her prey. Then the cold noise of steel against steel and a first lock fell to the floor, marmalade blonde against silky black. A pungent memory of ammonia rose from it, itched Rose's nostrils and made her eyes water. She squeezed them tightly shut, determined not to cry. She'd tried to explain, to tell Miss Behan how she'd come to buy the dye in the first place, but the teacher had demanded she be silent, had refused to listen, it was too late now. The searing sound of steel against steel came to her once more as Miss Behan cut a crazed zig-zag pattern high across Grace's scalp. It left a paleness visible in some places, tufts of orange dyed hair clumped together in others, while what remained of her long locks still hung limply to below her shoulders. Yet Grace stood erect and looked straight ahead in hopeless heroism, unbowed as any of the classics teacher's beloved warriors as they defended the pass yet again against the Spartans. A final cut, a last lock fell, then 'Miss Leahy, please', as Rose was summoned to the fore. She risked a glance at her friend as they passed each other, saw Grace give a brazen 'no regrets, see if I care' shrug as the assembled classes continued to watch in mesmerised silence. Rose squeezed her eyes shut against their cowardice, their collusion, when not one of them had spoken out on their behalf. She dimly sensed what they wanted, and expected, in almost eager anticipation, that she would break, plea for mercy, beg for Christian forgiveness, acknowledge that she was no better than a prostitute, a veritable Magdalene. The steel blades closed in on her neck, the sharp points edged towards her right cheek; she felt their sharp edges meet and cut, felt the first locks fall from her head to circle her desolately on the floor. Behan's shoes creaked again as she moved to her left side. The shears neared that ear, and made the meeting of blades sound louder still, again and yet again.

'This will be followed by three days' suspension.' Behan addressed the assembly loudly when she was done, scissors still grasped in her right hand. A gasp rose from below, the censure being the maximum time allowed. A faint awareness of a new future flitted across Rose's terrified mind. And a letter of protest from her father followed.

Miss Behan, Madam,

I have learnt with considerable disquiet of ... I regret that you're handling of this situation has left me with little choice but to remove my beloved daughter from your school …

A long weekly bus journey into the city and to another school followed; then the cram college where she would study science and higher maths, Behan's classics and its heroic quest forgotten. In time she would join the modern scientific world, and register at university to major in chemistry.

2

How to host a six-course dinner party for up to ten guests. Grace's elderly mother had insisted on her daughter's eighteenth birthday that she take a year-long homemakers course towards her role as wife and mother, and her daughter scowled as she dressed, and belatedly read through her class notes on doing just that. *Requisite table placements are glasses (Waterford), cutlery (Newbridge) and napkins (Irish linen).*

'Do you truly believe, mother,' she asked in her empty flat, 'that when I dream of a man in my life I dream of us like that? Yearn for a man who'll be enthralled by my ability,' she bent towards her notes again, 'to roll butter into small circlets, place them in a dish (must be shell shaped) and decorate them with a spring of parsley atop.' She scowled as she fastened her bra. *It is important,* she read on, *that the wife also learn to carve lest the occasion arise that the husband be too inebriated to do so.* Grace pulled on her slip, took her notebook with her then sat by the mirror. *She will also of course see that he is suitably attired to receive guests, shirt collars starched with Robin blue, ironed crease centre back, and socks,* this note was underlined, *must be black in colour, as only popes, communists and socialists wear red.* Lipstick too bright, damn, never get away with that. She selected a pale peach shade from the cheap selection before her, one that was better suited to her sallow colouring, and applied it to her lips. Damn them if they thought she would go along with all this and settle for being *gently pretty, with a minimum of cosmetics, as natural beauty, unadorned, is what is expected of a wife.* She glanced farther down the page as she ran a brush through her hair and learnt that *the newspaper might be offered to him, folded neatly and open at the pages that interested him most — business, if that were his main fascination, sport, were he interested in that, and, if neither of these appealed, at the political commentary or daily editorial. The newspaper might, if unduly creased, also be ironed.* Grace hurled the notebook to the floor.

This wasn't the life she wanted and she hated the next section on children even more. 'I don't want any,' she said aloud, and as her voice echoed eerily in the silent room she felt so alone that she rescued her notebook for company and read on in a dispirited way. *Nourishment*, emphasised and underlined several times. *Milk puddings that ensured snow-white teeth and healthy gums, a pint a day, mixed at times with tapioca, semolina, blancmange or even rice, and only if they failed to entice with the modern instant whip. All to be topped with a blob of jam, home-made of course, and from the family garden's blackberry, gooseberry, raspberry and crab apple supply.* Two more long and dreary years, how wearily they stretched ahead, until, when twenty-one, her mother had agreed, she could do exactly as she pleased. Such boring space until then when she would go on to acquire shorthand and typing skills. Gregg's shorthand (the girls from better homes preferred it to Pitman), where she would train to take as much as one hundred words a minute, which she could them transcribe back to typed English at a speed of forty.

And so, come her twenty-first year, Grace Donovan set out for work each day dressed in a neat two-piece suit and freshly ironed blouse, pert hat, immaculate white gloves and well-polished court shoes, as she joined the army of secretary clerk-typists that commuted to the city daily to man Dublin's vast typing pools, hers being at the newly established All-Products Ireland: Import-Export Ltd. And, come Saturday, as she had retained her love of music, she sang at the G&R local amateur musical society, while she sang each Sunday too with the local church choir. She also remained friends with Rose, one of the few female college students who'd taken science, and who lived in healthy squalor in a tiny flat close by the campus.

On reaching eighteen, Rose too had matured to being ... well ... attractive, for she was neither beautiful nor plain, and, unlike Grace, was never the sort whose appearance caused her to stand out in a crowd. For Rose was of medium height, and her hair, a light brown, was given to appear dull, as was her skin, being unfashionably pale. Hazel eyes were perhaps her best feature, for when she smiled they lit up her face.

'Don't touch,' she called as Grace entered her tiny, book-filled flat, 'don't mess up my filing system. I have one, you know, even if it doesn't look like that.' She lifted a giant pile of papers, glanced around, and then gingerly placed it atop a stack of books in the far corner. 'OK, let's see ... sit there. Yes, there.' She cleared the table of several journals, and plonked a jar of coffee before her friend. Instant. Grace winced, then winced again as the water added to it clearly hadn't been fully boiled. Rose sensed her rejection. 'You'd prefer tea? Don't have tea bags right now, I'm afraid.' An opened sugar bag on the table was quickly joined by a carton of milk, and finally a spoon. 'There are chocolate biscuits somewhere.' She rummaged in a high press. 'No, must have eaten them all last night. Was studying 'til two a.m. Exams in three weeks. I'm wrecked. Ah, at last. Marietta. If they're soft take them from the bottom of the package, they'll still be crunchy there. Well, how goes it?' She wriggled her fingers atop the table as if typing. 'Met Mister perfect husband import-exporter yet?'

'Don't want a husband, Rose, you know that, and you're going to do me a favour.'

'Sure, anything. But once the exams are over. Just wish I was more certain of what'll come up. I've devised maths formulae to predict the questions, it's based on those set over the last seven years. Pete thinks it's safer to go back ten, so I did that too, then averaged out, and am banking that my top fifteen will come up.' She drank from her coffee mug. 'Still nervous though about the practicals, especially the bio. Sorry, but I just can't think of anything beyond exams right now.'

'Who's Pete?'

'Don't look at me like that. Business studies, number cruncher too. Men, in the way you mean, don't exist here come May. Bit at odds with nature, but there you are.'

'Oh come on, Rose, there's more to life than what you can see at the end of a microscope.'

'Once the exams are over, yes. I desperately want to get honours.'

'I'm still a virgin,' confessed Grace. 'I'm determined to be rid of it, and soon.'

'It's called a hymen,' said Rose chattily, though she noted how Grace's voice grew fierce, and understood how she greatly resisted being considered old-fashioned and traditional, as all around her the virtues of her elderly mother's generation – humility, loyalty, duty – fast became the vices of her own.

'I've dreamt of that time,' Grace confessed, 'I've planned it, know exactly how I want it to be.' This was so, for when she did, it always happened with a brooding stranger, the air soft and balmy all around them, under the light cast from a honey-coloured moon in a star-filled sky to the sound of waves lapping nearby, accompanied by a grand operatic aria, preferably from *Carmen*. 'I need to go abroad,' she confessed. 'I mean, Dublin, what's here save rain, clouds and the familiar? There are flights now to Lloret de Mar. They're cheap, I can afford them, and you're coming with me.'

'What d'you need me for? Hardly to watch?'

'Shut up, Rose. Come on, you can't let me go about this totally alone.'

'We only watch microbes do it, kid. At the highest point on the evolutionary chain it's a private matter, and you best keep it that way, for many still believe it's a sin, and of the intrinsically evil sort. You want to be banished to the Magdalene Laundries for life?'

'I'll not be bullied by fears. Look, I have the money, I can loan you your fare, pay me back later from your summer earnings.'

'Grace,' she spoke slowly, 'watch my lips move. My exams are in three weeks.'

'Then I go there alone. I'm determined ...'

A side glance convinced Rose that she meant it. 'Don't do that,' she retorted quickly. 'OK, but in a month's time. I've pencilled in ten days then, just to sleep.'

'I'll book the holiday straight away, for two, and for a week.'

'I suppose you could do that,' Rose pondered slowly. 'I'll be exhausted though and not much company. And look, you've got to leave; I've got to get back to the books.' She gestured towards the door and poured herself more coffee as she spoke. When suitably caffeine-fuelled she studied until her bloodshot eyes could no longer read the pages before her. Then she went on her knees and prayed as she had from her childhood days. 'Please God,' she pleaded, 'let me succeed. I beg you who has a divine plan for my one life, a clear way mapped out that you, in your compassionate wisdom, wills me to follow. Please, please God let me pass my exams and so allow me fulfil your divine calling. I know it is your will that I help lessen the sum total of pain in this world, so help me succeed in my career as a hospital pharmacist to do just that. Be my guide that I may fulfil thy will.'

At the pool, Grace was first drawn to Juan's bright red t-shirt, Che Guevara's face and freedom message emblazoned on it in black. When she looked further she saw that he was tall and olive-skinned, that his sleek hair was coal black and his eyes a deep brown. She watched as he kicked his feet free of his brown flip-flops, lowered his floral shorts to reveal a tight pair of black togs, then climbed the high ladder to the top diving board. Grace watched as he walked to the board edge, saw his lean body arch then lean forward to reveal a line of paler skin, now visible at where his skimpy swim trunks met his narrow hips. She gave a sharp intake of breath, then saw him dive, watched his sleek body sing through the air before it cut knife-like through the water. She still watched as he went under and disappeared, waited for what seemed like forever until he surfaced again, and, to her joyous surprise, close by where she sat. He gave her a wide white smile, ran his hand through his hair and tiny droplets sprayed her bare legs. He stretched out his hand towards her; she smiled and took it in hers as they both laughed, as he lifted himself from the water and onto the edge of the pool beside her. '*Cuba libre?*' he offered.

'*Si, si,*' she agreed. 'I'm Grace, by the way,' she laughed.

'Juan.' He laughed too. She liked the way he pronounced her name, how he called her 'Gracia' as he handed her the glass, for the Spanish equivalent of her name made her feel European, continental, not Irish anymore, altogether different. They sat at the poolside as they sipped from each other's glasses, she from the long straw that protruded from his rum drink, and he from hers. Occasionally their heads touched, then their eyes met, and she stirred the liquid coyly with the small paper umbrella that the floating lemon slice offered atop their shared beverages. After, they swam together, hers a leisurely breast stroke, his a more powerful over-arm, then she watched from the pool as he climbed to the highest board and dived again, and his body sang through the air, sang as some great operatic aria. After, he bought a tapas lunch, and they shared the spicy food that burnt her mouth and hit hot against the back of her throat.

When the sun climbed higher and the day grew overly hot, they moved into the shade and set out two towels under a large umbrella and lay together there, her smaller pale hand warm beneath his long-fingered bronze touch. Come afternoon, they raced to the beach and she watched him ride the waves on a narrow board. She tried to match his skill but failed to do so, and surfaced from the salty waves to find him smile down at her, a pedal boat beside him. Their legs worked in unison as it carried them out into the bay, where they swam again, before they returned through the salty foam. '*Mañana,*' he whispered close to her ear, as the sun set, and she readily agreed. *'Mañana.'*

Will I get the honour? Rose woke at two a.m. to a throbbing headache from three *Cuba libre* as her mind raced and re-calculated the results she anticipated. Would she get through without having to repeat Dr Meaney's paper? The last paper she'd taken caused her to toss and turn – damn that lecturer who'd set an unexpected question, and damn her decision too to attempt it first, then cause her to leave the final answer, which she knew, unfinished.

It's a holiday, I should be enjoying myself, she thought as she glanced to where Grace slept peacefully in the second bed. Her shoulders hurt every time she turned, and the pink blotches around her strap marks ached. She should have brought more clothes too; two sets of shorts and three t-shirts weren't nearly enough for this heat, and the pile of washed clothes that lay abandoned in the sink couldn't be hung out on the balcony to dry. Forbidden to do that. She suddenly had a brainwave: Grace's hairdryer. She'd dry them with that, and buy a new pair of togs, the pair she'd brought were only fit for the bin. Breast uplifts hard from the wash in hot water, when the label she'd failed to read said 'wash only in cold'. God, how her sunburn ached. She'd definitely sit in the shade tomorrow and maybe read there. At least the library, whatever the hotel's limitations, boasted plenty of books. A Georgette Heyer (when men were gallant and love was true), or an Annie M.P Smithson (where love of man vied with love of country), what would she choose next? Once she'd finished the Maugham and Greene she'd brought with her from Ireland. And why was Grace's seduction of Juan taking so long when by page three hundred and nineteen of *Of Human Bondage* Philip was in no doubt that he loved the ghastly Mildred; and

Scobie's struggle between his Catholic god and Helen had raged on from the opening page.

Maybe, she glanced towards the sleeping Grace again, *I should go on a tour. Maybe my being around curtails their advances. Join a noisy coachload of Liverpudlians and take the steep climb with them to the monastery at Monserrat. Might even pray at the shrine of the Black Madonna there. Light a penny candle and pray again for exam success. I could even pray for that right now, might help me sleep. Mother Mary, grant me exam success. You who have a unique divine plan for my life, and you who,* Salve Regina, Mater Misericordiae *is forever merciful of human frailty and constantly intercedes on our behalf help me gain an honours grade. And Divine Mother, you whose blackness is of the earth, and you, who were also fully human, protect Grace.*

Grace strolled hand in hand with Juan along the sand, the warm air balmy against her skin. To her right she heard the pounding rhythm of the waves, the dark sea cloaked in moonlight. The sky was starless. To her left, and beyond the promenade, the disco they had just left continued, and when she glanced that way she could still see the revellers dance beneath the coloured lights that flashed about them. When they paused to kiss, she tasted the *Cuba libre* on Juan's harsh breath, and felt his tongue probe the inner recesses of her mouth. Once they found a deserted part of the beach they halted, and lay down together on the sands. He looked at her admirably, her pearl earrings cream against her skin, then slowly took one pink nipple between his lips and sucked it fiercely, pausing only to discard his t-shirt. Together for a time, naked to the waist, until he lowered his shorts and togs. His hard penis felt enormous as she took it in both her hands and stroked it, then he lay atop her. 'It is safe?'

'Yes.'

'You are sure?'

'Yes.'

'You say "yes" to me inside you?'

'Yes. Yes.'

They clung together naked, mouth to mouth, tongue to tongue, chest to breasts, penis hard against the soft crease between her legs. Moving, harder, faster, quicker until she felt him enter her. And, to her surprise, it hurt. He thrust forcefully high and hard up inside her, his body heavy upon her, and began to move up and down as if he'd suddenly forgotten she was there. Then he paused, cupped her face in both his hands and looked straight into her eyes. 'Be with me,' he whispered, his pupils brown and huge. 'Be with me, my Gracia.' They began to move rhythmically together, and Grace began to enjoy it again, heard his breath urgent and harsh against her ear, felt his lips find hers again, inhaled the salty sea smell from his dark chest. She clasped both her legs around his, grasped his round buttocks in both her hands and pulled him even farther up within her. His fingers found her nipple, pressed it again, and her pink tissue rose hard to his touch. They moved in unison again, in and out, out and in. He paused to delay his climax, then moved again. Then his right hand stretched down to between her thighs, and found the clitoris that rose hard there. She moaned deliciously as he began to caress it, heard him moan too as he continued to thrust inside her, until they finally came.

'The first time for you?' He held up long fingers, blood stained in the moonlight.

'Yes, and from the minute I first saw you I wanted it to

be only you.'

He kissed his blooded fingertips one by one, eyes filled with mute adoration. 'You are my woman now.'

She sighed in agreement. It had happened almost exactly as she had dreamt it.

Grace returned home elated. Rose too was pleased to discover she'd passed all her papers and secured an overall honours grade.

In February an east wind blew in from Russia. It carried snow with it that fell at night and froze, thawed to grimy slush come midday, then fell and froze again, in a cycle that repeated over several days with no sign of let-up. Those privileged to have central heating hurriedly checked their oil supply, the majority who didn't build giant coal and log fires, while those impoverished enough to afford neither huddled over storage heaters and two-bar electric fires. Of the homeless who slept out of doors, three froze to death.

Juan arrived. He stood at the door of Rose's flat attired in the same gear that Grace had found so irresistible on the beach at Lloret de Mar: brown rubber flip-flops, floral-coloured knee-length cotton shorts with a red t-shirt, Che Guevara's bearded face and freedom message emblazoned on its front. 'Rosa,' he croaked, 'I come for my Gracia.'

'Christ, Juan. Look, Grace is away, she's in Rosslare, clearing perishables and "very urgent" through our one open port.'

'My Gracia?' he pleaded through blue lips, 'home soon? Man next door tell me to come here to you.'

'Come in, I'll get you a towel and hot soup, I'll phone her for you.'

'Rosa, always very good friend, thank you, thank you.'

'Who? I'm up to my eyes, you've no idea of the pandemonium here, ships piled up back as far as Wales. Who? Juan? This your idea of a joke? Juan? He can't be, that's over, I wrote at Christmas to finish it.'

'What am I to do with him?'

There was a pause. 'There's a key to my flat,' she said at last, 'it's on the window sill, under the flower pot. Let him in with that. Keep an eye on him for me, will you? Until Sunday, I've to work all day Saturday, I'll be back then.'

'Tell me about your trip,' Rose asked as she handed him warm clothes – an Aran sweater, tracksuit bottoms, an old anorak – before setting about heating soup which he devoured with thickly sliced bread.

'Plane has to go to Belfast ...' he ate ravenously '...so bus to Dublin. Much customs. First stop three officers walk up and down the bus, they take smuggled goods, Mars bars, Maltesers, four people have too many, then, what do you say ... for sex ... condoms, six packs from three men, and two bad books from the girl who sits next to me. She cries and looks out window, says she is seventeen too, just as Miss O'Brien's *Country Girls*. Customs ask about my Che. I tell him I am Spanish but Che is my hero too; he grunts, he moves on. Second officer asks for passports then asks why I am here. I am afraid, but with officials best to tell truth, truth is no sin. So I say I am here to be with my Irish Gracia, girl I love. He moves on too. Drives on, beautiful snow outside.'

'You've never seen snow before?' Rose smiled.

'Once, very small, grandfather brings me up high into the mountains and I see it then. He says up there it is nearer to God.'

34

'Look, I'd love to stay and talk more, but I've a lecture at midday that I can't miss.'

'*Si. Si.* You leave now, and I wait for my Gracia. I see you again *mañana*? *Si?*'

'You were brutal.' Rose was angry, and Juan had returned to Spain.

'It's over. I wrote and told him so. Alright, how would you have handled it?'

Rose blushed. 'It wasn't my problem, it was yours,' she retorted quietly, for while Rose threw herself into her studies and into college life, a fear that love might never be hers occasionally surfaced for her and refused to go away. She had faced the painful truth that men would never be magnetised by her as they were by Grace, and it seemed to her that Grace had just thrown her precious chance of love away. 'He wanted to surprise you, thought you'd be delighted to see him. How could you?'

'He'll recover. Dumpees do, I believe.'

'He hoped to get work here, and if not, wanted you to return to Spain with him. What mattered to him was that you'd be together.'

'That was *never* in my plan.'

'Your *plan*?'

'Yes, my plan. And I was straight with him from the start. I wanted the first time to be exotic, not with some boozed-up business exporter at 3 a.m. in a grotty Dublin hotel. I wanted it to be ... well, just as it was. I'm determined to cling to ... never to forget that. That was my dream, he helped it come true, and I thanked him endlessly, honest. I never expected that ...'

'He'd fall in love with you?'

'You think he did?'

'Yes.'

'Oh. I need to think about that.'

'You'll marry, Grace. Not Juan. Just someone else.'

'Not for me. I'm so determined. You'll see. I intend to remain forever free to follow my heart. Marriage? You want me just to settle for being part of a tribe of women all being herded in that direction? No way. Doesn't mean I give up on sex though. Anyway, he was horrid at the end, didn't want to leave, swore at me and named me with all the whores of Christendom. Finally I just lied, said anything that might help me be rid of him. In the end I even promised I'd fly out to him again come summer though I've no intention of doing that. The lies at the end, that's what I hate most, when I wanted always to be straight, to be honest. I hate myself for them. Funny that I can't hate him as much as I do that, just hate and blame myself for selling out on that.'

3

Rose glanced towards Pete again as they left the campus and walked along the Blackrock road. She grinned. They'd known each other for almost four years now and what she liked most about him was the way he fitted in. Mandatory uniform of denims and sweatshirt, just like her own. Not at all like those who won firsts and awards and made her feel inferior, or the sport nuts who were worse still, or the promising artists who vied dramatically for attention, even during tricky experiments in the lab. True, his red hair and freckles made him stand out a bit, yet he'd declined to allow those carrot-coloured locks grow biblical-long (an absolute campus rage), and quietly decided that a monthly short back and sides still suited just fine. Rose approved strongly of that, but most of all cherished his ability to listen, when his quiet presence belied an astute grey-eyed gaze that suggested he missed little. And as they wove through the crowds she continued to chat, about their final exams, about her practical, at which she'd done well, the papers and questions she'd answered with confidence, the fear that her project would not gain the yearned-for honours grade. It was only when they neared the park that she paused. 'Look, I'm sorry,' she smiled, 'always going on and on, and always about myself. How are things with you?'

'I expect to pass,' he shrugged with pretend carelessness, 'and that's as much as I want anyway.' She already knew that to be so, had realised some time before that he put little emphasis on academic acclaim. Had taken a business degree for he looked instead for new, innovative ideas that might be applied in the marketplace. Well, she could hardly argue with that; as an almost-pharmacist she knew the value of original insights too. After Fleming, Pasteur, Salk. His, she expected, would be of a more mundane variety, of the business kind, the sort marketeers might take on board were they profitable.

'Look,' he steered her through the park gate, 'I need to talk with you about something more important than exams. I need to tell you ...' His colour heightened as he spoke and she looked up at him in surprise as he paused beneath a tree and stood over her. 'I woke three nights back,' he began, as she leaned against the bark, 'and realised I wouldn't see much of you anymore, and I couldn't bear it.'

'I didn't expect this.'

'I need you in my life. Be with me.'

'I don't know what to say.'

'Look, I know I don't have much of a chance. I mean, you're one of the brightest, always with high honours, when I seldom get any better than a pass.'

'But we were pals, good friends,' she protested. A myriad of memories suddenly came to her, of freshers' week, how he'd rescued her from a noisy crowd who'd jeered women registering for science. How he'd brought takeaways to her flat when she'd studied until two or three in the morning, put away the coffee mug and insisted that first she eat and then she sleep. He'd visited each time she took ill, brought medicines when she'd been laid low with flu, got the notes of the course lectures she'd missed. And what had she done in return? Taken it all for granted, thanked him briefly, and forgotten.

'Do I have any chance? I'm terrified I'll never see you

again.' He held her gaze and she looked up as if seeing him for the first time. She noted that he was taller than her, if only just, saw the pale hint of his need for a shave and the darker hairs that grew long on his arms, the thicker growth visible beneath his open shirt and matted on his freckled chest.

'Yes,' she whispered, suddenly shy.

'You've made me the happiest man.' Above them, an early summer sun shone through the dense blood thorn foliage and cast speckles of light around them both. Vibrant green leaves, their shapes indented, brushed her cheek, while above them a crimson cloud of red blossoms cascaded downwards, hiding the long, sharp thorns that grew beneath. Soon its blossoms would fall in tiny red petals and carpet the ground where they stood. Come autumn, its dense foliage would redden again, grow heavy with crimson haw berries, be gathered by some to make a luxurious berry wine. She felt him press against her, his breath on her lips, his tongue eagerly probing her mouth, and she tasted their very long, very slow first kiss. Then he held her close as they both laughed and laughed in amazed delight at their shared good fortune.

Everything changed. When Rose recalled the four previous years she now remembered them differently, as he came to the foreground in her recollections and what had once mattered over those student years faded to the background. She recalled him in a thousand ways she'd seldom noted before, situations where he now starred as near-hero permeated by warmth, by light. At the L&H, at those noisy Saturday debates, how he'd listened intently and seldom intervened, then made a succinct point that caused visiting speakers to glance his way in surprised interest. They'd marched together at the recent student protest. Had she even forgotten his kindness to that fresher who'd got a police baton; while all around protesters had shouted and screamed at the cops (she had too), it was he who'd paused to quell the blood flow that streamed down that terrified face. He'd even rowed for college the previous year when they'd won the Gannon Cup.

She'd been there; the repetitive and rhythmic sound of oar as it sliced through Liffey waters came to her memory once more as she yearned to be kissed again. So many such encounters tumbled about inside her delighted self, but of most significance to her now, of those four college years, was that *she* had met *him* there. And, over the weeks that followed, as they waited for their final results, and as they'd little money to afford much else, they tramped the Dublin hills each day together in summer sunshine. Crossed boggy terrain through yellow gorse and purple heather from the giant pagan monument at Three Rock to the pagan stones at Two Rock, and viewed the city far below them, its wide sweep of bay spread out beneath. They picnicked in that high place, shared sandwiches and beer, they lay in the heather through the afternoon and soaked up the light. On another day they made the steep climb to the ruins of The Hell Fire Club. She clutched his hand tightly as they entered that ruined place, for it was rumoured that ghosts of wild youths who'd gambled away vast fortunes still haunted it. They made their way up the broken staircase to the second floor, for despite Pete's company, its icy eeriness made her shiver.

'Do you gamble?' she asked.

'Will have to, if I'm to set up in business, there's always a gamble in that.'

'That frightens me.'

'Hold my hand, we may meet the cloven-hoofed devil greed on the way out.'

And she laughed, happy again.

On other days they walked the local beaches, by the long promenade at Bray, around the pretty harbour at Greystones, raced each other along the length of Brittas strand, then lay in the sand dunes together.

'Not everything,' she smiled, as he pressed her, 'not yet.' For despite her traditional values she was willing to permit him some sexual liberties, for he was special to her.

'Why?' he pressed.

'Look, I know the way you lads talk of women who give you a total "yes", —"second hand rose", "soiled goods" ...' her eyes grew angry as she spoke, '... "a free ride", "three gins and she's anyone's".'

'I haven't ever thought of you in that way,' he protested truthfully.

'True, but you've still got to wait.'

'Why? Don't you trust me?'

'I do.' She rolled away from him and brushed fine grains of sand from her skirt as she answered. 'What I don't trust is my fertile body. All those sperm of yours, thousands of them, racing upwards to win my one egg. When I read of that and saw sperm through my microscope for the first time I thought it was so incredible. But not just yet, thanks, I'm about to be a career gal.'

'We'd marry if we got caught that way. Look, trust me, I'll take great care, honest injun.'

'No, we don't risk starting our life together with a shotgun marriage.'

'You'll soon be a pharmacist, right?' he persisted. 'What

then? Will you fill illegal Irish prescriptions for the pill?'

'Don't try that one on me. And stop pretending this is about anything except your ... you know. I'm sick of the heated debates in the student pub on all that. And I don't believe that women who favour contraception hate children, or that feminists who object to the laws of an all-male church and state hate men. If they all did, what would they want contraceptives for? It's all bunkum. As for your question, the doctor prescribes, I fill. The ethical and moral choice falls on them, not me. What's more, I'm about to qualify as a pharmacist. A Catholic pharmacist ... there's no such thing.'

'That's a cop-out. How Catholic are you anyhow?'

'Enjoying this, aren't you, when all you want is ...'

'True. Worth a try though.'

'I believe what I was taught to believe at home and school. Haven't given it much thought since. I still go to mass each Sunday alright, and pray, especially coming up to exam time. You know, pray as if all depends on God, work as if all depends on yourself.'

'All gloriously scientific. How do you reconcile the two?'

Rose thought for a time. 'Well, it's a kind of apartheid, I suppose,' she replied slowly. 'They peacefully co-exist in separate compartments in my mind. Anyway, stop pretending you give a damn about any of this when all you want is ...'

'True. My needs are simple. Come on, say yes.'

She laughed, then lay back in the sun again, felt his weight as he lay atop her. 'But not everything.'

Then followed the exciting and fearful task of finding

work, subject to exam success ... Rose applied to all the city hospitals for work as a trainee pharmacist and secured three interviews. She accepted the first job offered her, at Saint Mary's (it required an honours grade and was one of the suburban hospitals south of the city), and prepared to begin work there on August 1st.

'What happened to the student I learnt to love?' asked Pete as she appeared in a pencil-slim skirt and neat blouse, hair neatly cut and coiffured.

'Will this look OK beneath my white coat? I need staff and patients to trust me.'

'I'd trust you with my most precious parts, anytime.'

His search was more complex as he was determined to set up in business on his own, within the food sector. Foods, vegetables in particular, were traditionally sold fresh or canned, but more and more people now owned fridges with freezer compartments. He planned to provide frozen vegetables and set about drawing up a business plan to that effect. The support he engendered was tenuous, and as the first three banks he approached turned him down, inner voices grew louder within him as to the hopelessness of his efforts. *The civil service offers good work, permanent and pensionable, you'd be much safer there. What could you know of business, we've no history of that in our family?* Was that his late father, who'd died when he was seven? *Try the banks for a job. Your cousin's doing well, in head office now, you'd do worse than follow on a career like his.* His uncle, who'd assumed an in loco parentis role following his father's premature death: *So you want adventure? Well, if that's the case, why not join the airlines? Good pay, cheap travel, and they've openings at administrative levels right now.* He didn't want safe, secure employment, he yearned to be self-employed, to set up and run his own business, and he grew weary of the naysayers. For no one encouraged him. No one save Rose. She believed steadfastly in him, and by so doing won his greater love. Rose, who in youthful naiveté placed little emphasis on financial security, backed him all the way. To follow his dream. And so made it possible for him to hold out until he finally found a banker prepared to finance him. He then quickly leased small premises and bought machinery, secured suppliers, developed a distribution network to shops and supermarkets, and explored issues around display and advertising. Only Rose knew how frightened, even terrified, he became at times.

'You'll succeed,' she whispered, 'I know you will.'

'I'm less sure right now. I've just run into another problem I didn't anticipate ...'

'Shhh. I know you can do it.'

'Do you?'

'Look, we can scrape by on my salary for a time if needs be.'

That was Rose. His one-day wife, best pal, soul mate, and dream maker.

Grace arrived at Rose's small flat to congratulate her on qualifying. She brought food. Little bits of dainties wrapped in napkins which she carefully laid out on the one clear part of the cluttered kitchen table. And while Rose, whose eating habits were timed to match her hunger and she hadn't eaten since breakfast, thanked her, she secretly wished she'd brought something more filling than the pretty array of tiny biscuits topped with selections of soft cheese, a stoned green olive, and a neat sprig of parsley each. Rose stifled a yawn and tried to appear interested as

Grace went to great lengths to explain how she'd managed to retain the crispness and saltiness in the small crackers even though the cheeses were of an expensively soft variety, and pretended to be delighted when she made a fuss of popping the cork of a snipe of bubbly, when she disliked champagne, which made her sneeze, and would have far preferred a beer.

'You start work when? Monday?' Grace raised her glass.

'Yeah, I'm a bit nervous, excited and nervous.' Rose bit into the savoury, felt the velvety taste of olive in her mouth, then raised her glass. 'Thanks for this. How's your own work going?'

'Better than I expected. You remember I was sent to Rosslare during the cold spell some time back? Well, the powers that be were impressed by the way I handled all that, and I've been offered a clerical position, out of the dead-end typing pool and on a track that at least offers promotion. At the end of the day, what really keeps me going is my singing. Did I tell you? I've joined the G&R, we're putting on *Oklahoma* at the Gaiety in November. You'll come?'

'Sure, count me in for two tickets. Pete and ...' She yearned to tell Grace her exciting news but Grace chatted on, oblivious to the interruption.

'Rehearsals two evenings a week, as many as four closer to the opening. I'm loving it, play Ado Annie. All the real-life sex is in the chorus though; they're a mass of heaving passions. Six romances, everything, from mild flings to "this is forever". We even have a scandal. I won't give you their names 'cause he's married and she's smitten *tragique*. Wife at home with three kids, and has no interest in music. How could he? No sex coming my way though. Could sing

45

of love together forever with our best baritone, bring a packed theatre to its feet: "more, more", standing ovations. But no real buzz between us. No, none at all.'

'Are you still too frightened to risk it again, I mean the way it all ended with Juan?'

'Me? Frightened? Me? I haven't thought about it in that way.'

'Think about what I've just said.'

'Maybe I should a bit. Am I being a bit unforgiving of myself? Yeah, I'll think about that.' She reached for another of her biscuits. 'Um, taste good, don't they?'

'Grace, I must tell you. Pete and I are ... well ... we're serious.'

'Pete? You mean Pete? Red hair and freckles Pete? Sweet Jesus, Rose. But you've known him for ages.'

'What's that got to do with it? He grew on me.'

'Nothing, I suppose, just don't think of love in that way maybe. Pete? It's hard to take in, that's all. Pete? He's nice, yeah, Pete's nice.'

'Nice! How could she. Nice! The most tepid word ever said.'

'We're in love,' Rose whispered, her voice low. She hid her disappointment at her friend's response. How could Grace, who loved music and love songs, who warbled *Lara's Theme* before she even scrubbed her morning teeth, believe that the length of time they knew each other had anything to do with it. 'To Rose and Pete,' she said quietly, then raised her glass.

Grace shook her head in amazement, then followed suit. 'To Pete and Rose.'

She graduated, one of the few girls who did so among a

large class of men. Had Grace not come to the church on that one day long ago would any of this have happened? No hair dye with which to thank her, no humiliating shaved head before the assembled school, no letter of protest from her father, no daily bus journey to study science in one of the few city schools that taught the subject to girls. She might have studied the classics instead and learnt of heroic quests, of how boys became men, men became heroes, and heroes became gods, of those who set out on brave quests, took great risks, finally succeeded and afterwards were immortalised. Instead she learnt nothing further of the ancient Greeks and their European Celtic cousins, of their triumphs and failures, save for an occasional soft echo that surprised her infrequently when it came to mind. For when talk was of a few who'd made a principled if hopeless stand, the Spartans defended the pass yet again, and when she read of a distant city that fell in war she recalled the women of Troy who'd waited helplessly for the barbarians to claim them as conquerors' booty. When someone brought inevitable and terrible news, she always counselled, 'Don't shoot the messenger.' And while she heard *Ag Chríost an Síol, ag Chríost an Fhomair* sung at Sunday mass, it brought her a melodic sound rather than any profound realisation of the strange challenge a belief in the divine presence in the natural order presented to Genesis and to Rome. For now she understood far better the principles that underpinned scientific research, intellectual discourse, how hypotheses were arrived at and how theories developed. And, at all times, their preferred numerical analysis suited her talents just fine.

4

Am I cruel? Grace pondered over and over, for Rose's accusation, given the anger in her friend's eyes, had thrown her. *Was it my fault that things ended with Juan the way they did? I certainly didn't plan it that way. Love's about pleasure, I gave him more than a little of that. He might at least have been grateful, instead of damning me with all the whores of Christendom. Was I cruel to Rose too? Maybe, but who in their sane senses could get excited about Pete? He's grown on her! Does she truly want a man who'll creep up on her slowly like some clinging vine? Yet what if I don't ever love again, have grown too fearful to do so?*

Such fears rankled and played repeatedly in Grace's mind, until she glumly realised one day that she needed Christian forgiveness, and it was in such a mind frame that she paused on her way home from work one evening at a city church, went inside, and found a priest who heard confessions at a small table by the main altar. He glanced at her, nodded, and then gestured to her to sit across from him, which she nervously did. A breviary, its ribbon marker red against the green baize table, rested beside a simple cross, and a purple stole with one cross embroidered with gold thread.

'What troubles you?' he asked, voice gentle.

The padre, his name unknown to Grace, was best known in clerical circles for his intellectual brilliance, and his posting as a lowly curate had been something of a surprise to his contemporaries. For Father Y held a master's degree from Louvain on an obscure if hotly debated passage in Aquinian canon law, and a doctorate in philosophy from Rome on the Thomastic tradition's influence on contemporary Christo-European thought. His posting, announced from the palatial home of Dublin's austere archbishop, had been made to foster humility in his soul, and to ensure his avoidance of the most cardinal of all sins, pride. A further reason, less frequently voiced, was that the young curate favoured Vatican II and, with his academic brilliance and Rome contacts, posed a challenge to the aging archbishop's policy of 'no change'.

Father Y, who had returned to Ireland eager to implement the new vision, found that he was squashed at every turn for his efforts. Nonetheless, he had managed to extricate some small gains: the Eucharist he gave by hand; his flock were invited for coffee and cakes after Sunday mass; and he heard confessions openly at a small table (as much counsellor as priest) rather than in the old-style dark boxes that terrified first communicants and evoked horror among his new-found Protestant allies. Yet after two years of forgiving the petty peccadillos of small-town provincials, occupants of the capital of a bog land on the periphery of Europe, he secretly yearned for the great libraries of Louvain, for the political power play at the heart of Catholic Rome, yearned too to forgive the powerful few of their great sins, to soothe the tortured struggle of a contemporary Thomas Moore, a great Henry, even a Beckett, but knew that in this small medieval parish none were ever likely to come his way. And while he tried desperately to show concern for the everyday travails of his humble parishioners, it pained him to acknowledge that none interested him much, save suddenly and unexpectedly the young woman who now sat across from him. Something powerful stirred his groin, an experience that left his celibate soul uneasy, particularly as it had happened in sacramental space, but he quickly cast the temptation aside and focused his thoughts on the great biblical story where his hero, the redeemer Christ man, came to mind, weary feet soothed by herbal ointments and gentle female caresses, then dried by the flowing locks of the Magdalene town prostitute. And across from him he jealously saw in Grace's trusting gaze that of the first one to witness the resurrection, vibrantly alive in his proximity, voluptuous as Reni's penitent, magnificent as Caravaggio's saint-whore.

'I haven't asked your name,' he said quietly, in surprised relief that his words came in a voice that was ordinary, even mundane.

'Grace,' she whispered in the empty church. 'Grace Mary,' she continued lightly. 'I took Mary for my confirmation name, but everyone calls me Grace.'

'What troubles you, Grace?'

She told him. Her voice stumbled at first, then grew more confident as he listened and occasionally nodded.

'You are forgiven,' he said when she had finished, and reached for his stole. She watched patiently as he kissed the embroidered gold cross, saw his youthful lips pressed against it, waited as he placed it around his neck, until it hung, regally purple, on his chest against his black shirt. 'I absolve you.' He raised his right hand to bless her. 'In the name of the father,' he began, 'and of the son ...' he paused '... and of the holy spirit.' She bowed her head. 'Amen,' he concluded.

She was healed, forgiven, and the fear that her past cruelties might limit her capacity to find love again vanished. She raised her eyes to meet his gaze and as she did so the same hand that had recently blessed her slowly reached across the table and covered hers. A hand that was long and slim, its youthful skin slightly tanned to tapered fingers, and neatly cut nails. She felt his physical caress, his bodily touch, and knew immediately that they wanted each other.

His voice grew casual. 'We have a drop-in centre each Sunday. Join us,' he suggested with pretend indifference. 'Why not join me come Sunday next, we might even share a sandwich over lunch.'

'I'd like that,' Grace agreed, then left.

Three weeks later they became lovers.

After each coitus Father Y castigated himself for his breach of his vows of chastity and of the celibacy ruling. Not for him the physical whip (he was not of the Opus Dei mould), but rather a cerebral verbal chastisement, as he applied his fine theological mind to his own errant sinfulness. He had fallen again, and once again was damned before his all-powerful God. He tossed and turned in his narrow celibate bed as he engaged in dark hours of moral struggle, and finally greeted a weary dawn. Only then, at first light, did he find biblical assurance that the good man fell seventy times a day, that his father God was merciful and full of compassion, his compassion wide, wide as the ocean, and that Christ-like, he too might rid himself and his Magdalene of her lustful demons. He slept briefly then and come morning woke strangely refreshed, confident again and full of sinful pride that he could of course resist temptation, and see that Grace did too. Which he did, but only while Grace remained outside his radar. Which she never did for long. For Y, in his struggle, generated an irresistible intensity of energy (to be envied by the more jaded palettes of sophisticated fleshpots) as his obsession with their sexual transgressions blazed as petrol to flame. For the more forbidden Grace was, the more powerful she became. Indeed, Y had raised a modest grade-three clerk typist of moderate good looks to the level of Christianity's great whore-saint, one whose beauty and sanctity was of great cathedrals named, one who had survived almost two thousand years of celibate history.

While Father Y's struggle was with his immortal soul and its sinfulness, Grace's was with her youthful and mortal body and its fertility and the terror of a crisis pregnancy. Y could not countenance contraceptives; to him they were sinful, and to purchase them was premeditated sin, while his fine grasp of canon law assured him that without premeditation, to occasionally be merely carried away in passion was considerably less heinous a sin, a less horrific crime. Grace, who knew little of the finer points of theology, and nothing at all of canon law, would cheerfully and secretly take the pill, but the pill and all contraceptives were also illegal, and save for a few Protestant doctors who looked after their own in Protestant hospitals, and a handful of liberal medics prepared to risk their careers in Catholic institutions by prescribing for wives for whom pregnancy might be fatal, it was, as far as she knew, unavailable. Her main source of information was the media, where she read horror front-page sensational accounts – one of a man, a respected professional, who'd been dragged through the district courts for attempting to smuggle two dozen condoms through Dublin airport, another of a woman, a God-fearing Catholic and mother of seven whose intercepted personal post had been found to contain an illegal diaphragm and gel. And of Mary Bourke Robinson, the young Ballina lawyer whose Senate bill had attempted to make contraception legal and had been defeated.

So Y, who, to be fair, had no wish to impregnate Grace in passionate sinfulness, developed a pattern of love-making, the ancient *coitus interruptus*, by which he withdrew before he spilt his seed, at times in her hand where it felt sticky against her palm and between her fingers. On other occasions on her naked belly where it trickled down and dried cold above her soft pubic hair, but never, being a bright biblical scholar too, as Oman was, on the ground. At times Y did avoid her, and over the two years that followed, Y's patterns of sanctity and sinfulness, of his personal fall and redemption, merged with the cycle of the Christian year. Y, in penitential mode, avoided seeing Grace throughout all of Lent, the season of abstinence, and again throughout November, when he remembered only the dead. After two quick encounters in early December, he also remained unavailable to her throughout Advent, as well as its lead-in to Christmas. Grace, on her part, stayed away from him over the times she was most fertile, which was midway within her menstrual cycle. But during each meeting outside of these times, so hopeless, so secret, so precious, their obsession with each other and the intensity of their love-making knew no bounds.

And so their relationship continued, as their interwoven lives revolved too around more ancient and primitive cycles of the earlier Celtic nature gods and goddesses. For Father Y's life centred on the life of his incarnate Christian God, who linked back to the more ancient belief in a sun god, light-bringer to the earth. And so to a daily cycle of light-darkness-light that centred on a celebration of mass, the re-enactment of Christ's blood sacrifice – while Grace, who carried a terror of pregnancy, grew obsessively aware of her menstrual cycle. Linked then, and more consciously so, back to the moon goddess monthly cycle, the five moonless nights when the ancients believed that the absent moon bled, and to the quarterly new moon that shone so powerful as to influence the ebb and flow of the earth's mighty oceans. Would she bleed this month? She was late again, would her period ever come? And how intensely relieved she was when it finally did.

During her third abstentious Lent, Grace determined to free herself from her hopeless obsession and explored Dublin life in search of a more suitable mate. Towards this end, she acquired a wardrobe of skimpy miniskirts, tank tops and very high heels, stocked up on cosmetics, including eye shadow and the palest of lipsticks. And, so equipped, she engaged in a forty-day exploration of what the city's nightlife might offer her. Over those weeks she jived wildly to Hurricane Johnny and the Jets and spun crazily to hucklebuck for Dave Kane and the Cats, spent Saturday night with rugby hopefuls at Lansdowne pavilion, and Sunday evenings at their mortal rivals in that same sport, at Belvedere. The following weekend a work colleague suggested the National might better suit her musical style, and she sedately waltzed several hours away with rural folk there. She also briefly took in the student dances, the Ags and Civil Chems, danced reels and jigs at the teachers' club and made several rounds of the singing pubs at the Abbey Tavern and O'Donoghue's. She met men at them all, young men, shared a chaste mineral with some, a beer with others, and on one occasion was offered, but declined, some pot. One guy who sang 'Carrickfergus' well at the Tavern where she had sung 'Raglan Road' wanted her, but while she liked him, she didn't want him.

'We could …' he'd said, when he eventually got her alone.

'Thanks, but I'm not ready for that just yet.'

'I'm willing to wait. Could we meet …?'

'Thanks, but not right now.'

'OK, that's OK. But why? We could make all sorts of music together. Don't go, I want to see you again.'

'No, I mean it. I'm not playing flirtatious games, honest.'

'OK. Look, I take in 5 a.m. mass on the quays before going home for shuteye. Want to join me, we could go together there?'

'Alright,' she agreed grudgingly. 'We could do that.'

He drove her into the city and held her hand as they strolled down the Liffeyside and into the dawn. Mass? The ritual reminded her so much of *him* that she wanted to weep. She glanced at the youth beside her, suddenly aware that the very energies he was eager to evoke in her were exactly those from which she struggled, in futility, to escape. She left him at the church gate and they didn't meet again.

Over that same Lent, Y withdrew from the world to consider his position, absented himself from his parish and went to live in a sheltered monastery in rural Kerry. There he shared the life of the contemplatives, slept in a simple cell that offered the minimum of comfort, shared their sparse rations, and joined them in prayer. In time, their silence soothed and their daily chants calmed, and his pace, as he walked the stone floor of the ancient cloisters, grew slower and more measured, and in that environment, a place where Grace had played no part, he missed her less. But he knew he had to choose and, in penitential mode and after much time spent in prayer and preparation, he made his way in a small boat to Skellig Michael where he climbed the steep steps to what remained of that ancient monastic settlement there atop its high sea rock. Once there he renewed his celibate vows, and once again renounced the world, the flesh and the devil as her temptress voice finally floated from him. 'If this be civilisation,' she mocked, 'I can give it a miss.' And the sacred music that she so loved too was also lost to the screams of seagulls, the winds that wailed all about him, and the Atlantic waves that crashed so far below.

Shortly after, in the knowledge that his calling was of service in the world, he returned to his parish. Once there he missed her again like some demon-ridden Magdalene who haunted him and whom, after four years of sinful indulgence, his insanity had permitted to become an intrinsic part of his inner life. And despite his best efforts he sought her out from among the congregation that attended Sunday mass or sang in the choir or approached him for communion, from those who paused to shake his hand at the church door or came to the presbytery after for tea and cakes. But she was never there. At times he started at the sight of some youthful woman who bore but a passing resemblance to her, and as that ancient yearning flooded his being yet again, he shook his head sadly on finding it wasn't she. He toyed with the idea of phoning her, and sometimes, busy at his desk, found his hand wander to the receiver, lift it and place it to his ear, but then, on hearing the familiar buzz, replaced it in its socket. He went so far as to dial once, but on the first ring he replaced it quickly. Finally, one cold evening he phoned her number again and permitted it to ring until she answered.

'Hello,' he said. He heard her surprise intake of breath, then silence. 'I just needed to hear your voice. How are you, Grace?' Soft sniffles that told him she wept. 'Please don't, I can't bear to think I've upset you so.'

'I'm pregnant,' she whispered, then put down the phone.

Grace lay on the narrow bunk in the small cabin. The movement of the ship made her stomach heave and she struggled wearily to the bathroom again and retched into the basin, a dry retching that produced no vomit and did nothing to alleviate the nausea inside her. She sat on the toilet for a time, felt the ship rock beneath her, then went to the basin and retched again. How dog tired and weary she felt for sleep that wouldn't come. The porthole suggested a blast of cold air, so she opened it and peered outside, dark sea below, black sky above, then returned to the cabin, and past Rose who slept calmly in the far bunk. Terror that she lacked the money to cover all her abortion costs gripped her again and she checked her wallet as she totted the expenses in her head. Return ticket, at least that was paid for, transport to the clinic and the costs there, anaesthetist, surgeon, nursing and medical care, board the night after, already booked nearby, followed by the return trip to the port again. The credit union manager had readily agreed to her request for an overdraft to purchase clothes, though he'd been adamant that it took two to three weeks to process such a request. Routine stuff, no problem, but the paperwork always took that long. Rose, in whom she'd eventually confided in desperation, had lent her what she needed, and had also reluctantly decided that her friend couldn't possibly travel alone and so had offered to accompany her. While her priest lover … No, she didn't want to think of him yet again, he'd …

'You expect *me* to fund your murderous destruction of an innocent life?'

She struggled to block that memory and her final encounter with him, yet it insisted on playing once again in her mind, just as it had played over and over since that night, played as some nightmarish tape that she feared would never cease.

'Who knows about it?' he'd asked immediately, his eyes suddenly fearful. 'Who have you told? They'd been in his car, parked up the usual byroad, where they'd made love intensely and secretly so many times previously.

'No one,' she'd lied, frightened of his anger. 'I've told no one.'

'The doctor? The nurse who carried out the test?'

'I refused to name the father,' she'd lied again.

'Good.'

He'd believed her, sounded relieved, then had gone on to address their problem as if it were distant, their many nights of pleasure now banished to the outer edges of memory, regrettable encounters that he now viewed from a distant cerebral place and with some distaste. To her their dilemma was immediate, as intimate as the urine she'd recently submitted for testing and that had confirmed she carried his child, as much part of her as her menstrual blood that for two periods now had steadfastly refused to flow.

'The solution is −' he spoke as he did at their first encounter, as a kind pastor and the good shepherd he modelled himself upon, suitably concerned for a parishioner he knew, if not at all well, '– that you go away for a time, have the child, and give it up for adoption.'

'I could have it and keep it. We might …' She had, in desperation, even nursed fantasies of them as man and wife, together with their beloved child. 'You could leave.'

'I will not live out the rest of my days ostracised as some spoilt priest.'

'You're not even prepared to consider it?'

'I have thought about it, Grace. Over Lent I considered my position and made my choice then. You will have your child and have it adopted.' He put the car key in the ignition as he spoke and went to turn it, but she grabbed his keyring and held the cold metal tightly in her hand.

'Grace? Really? Do you have to?'

'*My* child? It's yours too. And you want me to go through all of pregnancy, and labour? Have you any idea what that would be like, only to give the child away and never see it again? I can't face into that.'

'Pull yourself together, Grace, I'll see that you have support.'

'I believed you all the times you said you loved me.' The headlights of an approaching van lit them up suddenly, thundered noisily past, then their car darkened again.

'We can't stay here much longer. What's more, I still have a sermon to prepare for tomorrow. My car keys.'

'No. You'll hear me through.'

'I did love you once,' he conceded. 'Well, in a manner of speaking. Still do, if not that way anymore. It has to end. But to assure you of my concern I will arrange for the good nuns to look after you.'

'No, don't even suggest that. I'm not going into one of

those homes, no way. You want me to end up working in a laundry all my life?'

'Don't shout, you sound increasingly like a common fishwife.'

'I will have an abortion, because if you won't name our child as yours there is no other way.'

'Hear me. You won't do that. I will not countenance it. The slaughter of a total innocent, a vulnerable child. How can you even consider it?'

'I'm only nine weeks. It's far from being a child yet. Anyway, whose womb is it?'

'Abortion is murder, you know that. Grace, give me the keys.'

'War is murder, and you allow for just war at times. Why then is there never a just abortion?'

'Grace,' he said wearily, 'these debates are not for young women, these matters are decided by learned church fathers, and you and I are both bound by their teaching. Believe me, the nuns are totally discreet, your child will be found a good home with fine Catholic parents.'

'The child, the child, always the child. What about me?'

'The child is helpless, innocent, you are not. Nonetheless you'll be given support and shelter, be allowed to recover from the birth ...'

'And if you're so concerned about your child, how then can you give it away? It's your child as much as mine.'

'How can I be sure it's mine?' he snapped. 'Look, I see no point in—'

'You're accusing me of—'

'Shhh, keep your voice down.'

'How can you? I've not been with anyone else since we met.'

'No, you're not to blame. You were once innocent too, as innocent as the child you now carry, until that wretched Spaniard.'

'You're jealous of him?' she hit back. 'That's it, isn't it? Why, when I haven't seen him for an age?'

'Look, you're frightened, I understand that. Trust me and I'll see that you're signed out from the convent after six months or so. It will provide a sanctuary for you, a safe place in which to birth, away from scandalous gossip. Then you will be permitted a period to recover, followed by some weeks for repentance, after which you may leave. Trust me.'

'Repent?'

'Grace, I will repent too. We both must do that.'

'They'll cut my hair, that's part of what they do, isn't it?'

'What does that matter? Only for a time.'

'No, no, they won't do that.' She didn't know why that suddenly angered her so, could not make sense of the sudden surge of fury she felt and the childhood memories that flooded into her mind with it. She closed her eyes as she found herself before the school assembly once more. A large mass of students stood beneath her. Mary Jones was there, she remembered her face clearly, third in from the second row. Mary who liked art and painted well, the Jones girl who afterwards had … Mary's voice came to her clear as if she was close by.

They cut my hair too, I remembered when it was done to you, said it made me sinful. I had to wear a scarf in church after, even when I was bald, lest I tempt the priest. When the child came they took him from me straight away, said I wasn't the sort of girl you could leave a child with, said the nuns would be a better mother to him. I used to sneak upstairs on my way back from the laundry each evening, even held him for half an hour or so, one of the younger nuns was a bit kind and she pretended she didn't notice me there. He was a nice little fellow, he'd even begun to smile at me. Then I went up as usual one evening and found him gone. They'd given him away to others. I cried then, it was the first time I'd done that since it happened, up 'til then I wouldn't have given them the satisfaction of seeing me upset. After that I just didn't care much. No, I didn't try to escape. Katie, who I knew there, had tried to run away, but the cops found her after eight hours and brought her back. My mother came to see me once, and I begged and begged her to take me out of the place but she couldn't sign me out being only a woman and my father wouldn't because of the shame of it all. Mam promised me that she'd see that my brother would sign me out and he did, once he was an adult. She kept that promise. I never go home, but still see her secretly now and then. She's always fearful that my father'll find out, he's not ever to know that we meet.

'I will, as your parish priest, make the necessary arrangements for you.'

'No. No way.'

'Don't shout at me. There is no other way. Fifth: thou shalt not kill.'

'What if I also kill the God that would treat me so?'

'The Christian God is all-forgiving, he endlessly forgives you and me our sexual sins. What you plan is premeditated murder.'

'So God will forgive me, but what if I can't forgive him?'

'Really, Grace, you talk such dangerous nonsense. You'll never leave our church. How could you ever do that when you love our music so much?'

'Suppose so,' she conceded.

'Fine. And I have a sermon to prepare, so that is arranged.'

'Your keys.'

Back inside her small flat she faced herself in the mirror. A pale face and hollowed cheeks gazed back at her. 'You,' she said, choice made, 'will have an abortion.'

'Ten weeks?' the second doctor asked. He sat at a wide desk and she waited nervously as he read down through the file that the nurse had handed him. She was glad when that same nurse's hand rested reassuringly on her shoulder. 'All the prerequisite tests, nurse?'

'Yes. All documented there.'

'And Dr Kemp's report?'

'In the second section.'

'Of course.' He read through the file slowly, and each turn of page made a slight noise in the otherwise silent room. 'I need to ask you some personal questions,' he said at last. 'Confidentiality of course is assured.'

'Yes.'

'Twenty-five years old, I see. And single? I understand too that this, your first pregnancy, was unplanned?'

'Yes.' Her voice remained steady but she kept her eyes downcast as she replied.

'PFI,' added the nurse helpfully, and Grace felt her hand press her shoulder again.

'Pregnant from Ireland. Do you know who the father is?' he asked gently.

'Oh yes,' Grace replied quickly, alarmed that the question inferred that she'd been with innumerable men. 'We ... we've been to-together for almost f-four years,' she stammered. 'I wasn't with anyone else over that time.'

'And you've told him of your pregnancy?'

'Yes, he knows.'

'He's accompanied you here?'

'No, it's over between us now.'

'Finally? You're sure? After such a time, perhaps, with such unexpected news, he needed to get used to the idea. Is he single too? Might you marry yet?'

'Yes, he's single, but no, there's no hope of that now. He wants me to have it, though.'

'I see.' Her reply seemed to irk him. 'He wishes your pregnancy to continue but offers to play no role whatever as natural father. I see.'

'It's because he believes abortion is murder,' she confided, then lowered her eyes.

'Partner/father harbours ideological objections to termination.' She watched the black ink flow from his fountain pen across the white page, then saw him press the ink dry on the desk blotter beneath it. 'Your partner's moral beliefs are a private matter for him,' he continued dismissively. 'Be assured that my role involves no moral judgement of you whatever; rather, it is for me to make a medical recommendation on grounds of your health.'

'Oh.' She glanced up at the nurse. 'I thought that I could have an abortion on demand here.'

'No surgical procedure is ever granted by a medical practitioner on demand,' he explained, and she felt the nurse's hand tighten on her shoulder again as his voice grew testy. 'Money up and we'll do anything, is that what yours believe of us over here? No, nurse, allow me to explain. We, as doctors, do not apply any medical or surgical procedures to you, or to any patient, on so-called

64

demand. I assess you, make a diagnosis, followed by a recommendation based on your health. Clearly you've been under considerable stress, and I can, having considered all your test results and my colleagues' reports, recommend a termination on grounds of your mental health.'

Mental health? The term frightened her. Being pregnant, a state for which she had no desire but otherwise viewed as natural, as commonplace, had now placed her in a strangely terrifying world where her once lover had accused her of murder and the doctor who sat across from her feared for her very sanity. 'You think I'm mad?'

'Of course not.' He glanced at the nurse, who shook her head too. 'Clearly you've been under undue stress. And stress is not at all good for your health.' He closed the file and handed it back to the nurse. 'Talk with her after, will you, about more reliable contraception.'

'It's over between us. I won't need anything like that.'

'Of course you will,' he smiled. 'You're still a young woman. I've every confidence that you'll meet someone else in time. Nurse will continue to look after you from here.'

'If wrong there is, it is the lesser wrong,' Rose told herself fiercely yet again as she sat in the clinic's waiting room. On the far wall the clock ticked morosely on. Gone for over an hour now. The nurse had said the procedure was a short one, so why wasn't Grace back on the ward yet? She went to the beverage machine, pressed the button for tea, and watched the liquid gush out into the paper mug, black and strong, quickly followed by sugar and finally milk. Rose took a large swallow, then returned to her seat.

The doctor had explained that there was always some risk, however slight, with an anaesthetic. Had something gone wrong? She took a second gulp of tea. What if Grace haemorrhaged? Women sometimes did in these situations. What if she became seriously ill? What if she died? What might Rose do then? Grace wouldn't die, she was being ridiculous, yet what if their trip became public knowledge? Thinking of that, she grew alarmed again as to what assisting an abortion actually meant. Did that just apply to the medics who lived safely in England, or might it include her too who had provided money so as to make her trip possible? And accompanied her. Would she then, as chemist, ever get work in a Catholic medical service again? She pushed those thoughts hurriedly away, determined that no one would ever know.

Father Y certainly wouldn't talk – well, other than under the confessional seal – and certainly not Grace, and she hadn't told Pete, had presented it to him as a shopping trip, although she suspected he may have guessed. Pete wouldn't talk either. Or would he? She suddenly felt unsure, fearful of loosened male tongues after several pints. No, Pete wouldn't do that, she could trust him. She lifted a newspaper from the low table before her, determined to read it and focus on just that. The front page had a photo of Wilson as it told of another wildcat strike; electricians had downed tools and walked out yet again. Followed by much thunder on Britain's loss of competitiveness, with quotations attributed to several weighty Eurosceptics. The women's page was in lighter vein, and advised how she best amuse her children through summer with a museum and gallery trail (should it rain) or hurdy-gurdies with a picnic in Battersea Park should the sun shine. And finally the sports section, three full pages on the dejection of Arsenal fans who had lost again, followed by another two of supreme English confidence that they'd win the Ashes, though it didn't look like that to Pete who knew for sure that they didn't have an earthly. She cast it aside, rooted in her purse for sterling coins, and bought yet another cup of tea.

The clock ticked on and she thought again that she might go to reception to enquire; maybe they were busy and so had forgotten to inform her that Grace was back on the ward. Yet she drew back from doing that. 'PFI', the nurse had called as Grace had registered, and several staff members had looked towards them. She'd wanted to shout, 'It's not for me, I'm not the one who ...' but she was glad now that she'd remained silent. She'd wait another twenty minutes or so, then go to reception and ask.

She made her way outside to the grounds to clear her head. Walked down the side of the lawn, past the neat flowerbeds, beyond where the gardener was watering, and leaned against a huge, ancient tree that grew tall there. Beyond the wide gates life continued: cars that sped up and down interspersed by high red buses, pedestrians walking past, housewives with shopping bags, youths on their way to football practice, the elderly walking their dogs. It all looked so commonplace and ordinary. After a time, she went back inside.

'She's awake,' the nurse smiled, 'and back on ward. You can see her now.'

'She's OK?'

'Sure. Everything went fine.'

She walked quickly to the ward.

'How are you?' Grace's face was pale, her eyes closed.

'Relieved. I'm glad it's over. They said I can leave in an hour or so.'

'I'll call a taxi.'

'I'm sure I can walk.'

'Taxi to the boarding house, we return to Dublin tomorrow.'

'Rose, I want you to know something.'

'Shhh, not now.'

'I'll never, ever see him again.'

Rose nodded. She knew she meant it. She knew something else too. She had never met him, was never likely to, but how she hated him.

5

It was evening, the hospital quiet, the elective surgery for the day completed and the night medications distributed. Rose continued to take stock diligently.

Vaccines. The child clinic had been held that afternoon and was now over and she noted what had been dispensed, listed the returns on her stock sheet and then smiled, pleased that her tots had balanced. She loved that aspect of her work for it brought to mind chubby and healthy children no longer at risk from those once great killers, safe from the infected raw throat of diphtheria, the deadly measles rash, the ominous swellings that suggested mumps, the rubella that promised deafness, and most recently, the wasted and callipered polio limb. Clear writing too, a nurse's of course. Why did penmanship deteriorate the higher one climbed the medical hierarchy? She had learnt to read the doctors' expressions more speedily than she could read their writing – the consultants, those who pushed their way ahead and jumped all queues; the on-the-way-up docs, still courteous if abrupt; and the juniors who treated her as an equal colleague and if their ward was quiet occasionally lingered to chat. She glanced towards the clock: fifteen minutes yet before she handed over.

Antibiotics next, heavy draw on them as always. The busy medical wards boasted two prescribers, neither of whom could write clearly: Wyndham who favoured a more traditional approach, and a new arrival eager to include the newer brands. She'd heard them argue on this topic, for the older consultant could remember those TB homes, the long, narrow wards that boasted low windows and airy balconies, could still recall the rasping coughs and blood-streaked mucus, and the pleading eyes of his own doomed son. 'Our sympathies, sir, we are all truly sorry. We had hoped ... Thank you for your efforts, if all to no avail. My wife and I thank you.' How loyal he still was to those early cures, had less time for what he saw as the fancy newer brands. Save for syphilis, for which he was prepared to prescribe the latest drugs to the aging prostitutes from the city's canal banks. They *had* to finish out the course of pills he prescribed, even if their symptoms eased. When would they ever learn that?

Anaesthetics accurate, seldom a disparity there. Pain numbed now prior to all surgical incisions, the wild screams of trench amputees long forgotten except by a few aging First World War widows in long-stay geriatric wards and given to ramble on about the past. Five terminally ill there, and she still had to check the morphine drips, with no certainty as to how much longer the aged might linger, and now, unlike their once youthful husbands and lovers, granted a near pain-free death. It frustrated her to find that her numbers were out on the antiseptics. She glanced down through the accompanying notes ... ah yes, three bottles broken, that explained it. Lister, how she revered him higher than all the other forefathers of modern pharmacy, acclaimed him as her first secular saint. Father of antiseptics and antiseptic surgery. For she knew her roots; scratch the surface and a mere two generations back find a dank, overcrowded Dublin tenement, breeding ground for the killers dysentery, bronchitis and pneumonia.

Safe childbirth too. She smiled quietly and thought of Pete; at some distant and future time she'd have that. Until then ... there was the discovery of the Irish-American John Rock. She held the controversial pill package in her hand — illegal, save as a menstrual cycle regulator. She thought of Pete again, then shook her head. No, well at least not yet.

'Hi, you can sign off, I'll take over now.'

'Sorry, didn't see you come in. Thanks.'

'Anything unusual?'

'No. Looks like you'll have a quiet evening.'

'Great, brought a book.'

'See you again.' Rose grabbed her coat and left. Outside, her path was blocked as two ambulances pulled in, sirens blaring, blue lights flashing. She shook her head as she glanced back. Some quiet evening. A full bus passed down the road outside, followed by a second that failed to stop, and then a third rumbled up empty but out of service. They travelled in convoys, Rose sighed, as she began to walk home.

Inside her small flat was a kitchen sink still full of dishes, a clothes bag packed full for washing and an ironing basket full to overflowing. She plugged in the kettle, found a teabag, cleared a space on the crowded kitchen table and sat down to read again through Pete's business file. About to set up his own business. At last. She flicked through the file on international studies, Irish studies, towards a feasibility study and a business plan, drank more tea and then applied herself to read systematically and slowly through it.

American consumer surveys. Their recent returns predicted an ongoing boom market for frozen vegetables, supported by rising sales figures for the new trunk-size freezers, a growing number of which now occupied the more affluent garages of south Dublin homes. So far, so good. 'Begin with peas, broccoli, carrots', Pete had scrawled in the margin. 'Local competition?' Rose wrote in, handwriting small and neat beside his.

Initial Irish returns. She read down through the next paper, scoring what she saw as the most pertinent points made, as she'd learnt to do as a student, then read back later over what she'd underlined. While it seemed certain that frozen vegetables could pose a strong threat to the tinned variety, the jury was still out as to whether they could compete with fresh food in season. The CD class, who bought tinned, could not yet afford freezers, and the AB class, well, would they shift? And if not, would the return on frozen over, say, an eight-month (no fresh available) year be enough to make the venture profitable?

Numerical analysis. Rose, more at ease with figures, sighed with relief when she came to that. The report suggested that it would succeed, subject to an annual growth projection of two percent or more. Growth projections ... but then, how reliable were they?

Irish product resistance analysis followed. She drank more tea, then read down through it in growing dismay, saw that it drew attention to the Irish being newly industrialised, still close to their rural roots and so were 'different' from their mainstream British and Euro-American counterparts. Irish consumers, it suggested, offered a home market far removed from the shopping practices of those surveyed in international studies, those who came from the great urban centres whose forebears' trail had blazed the industrial revolution a century before. Their own, Rose nervously realised, still wanted their veg 'fresh', even, as one respondent suggested, with mud still clinging, for that provided irrefutable evidence that the product had just been pulled from the soil. Mud with food posed a congruence that alarmed Rose's antiseptic-loving mind. And women, who traditionally still carried out 97.34 per cent of the grocery shop, doubted that a frozen product contained as much nutritional value as fresh, and Rose ticked with her pen in agreement.

An 'attractive features' adjective list followed. What was most highly rated were frozen vegetables that were both 'nutritious' and 'fresh', the two friendliest adjectives that occurred repeatedly in the survey's returns. So different from the American obsession with 'speed', 'timesaving' and 'convenience', characteristics that offered little attraction for Dubliners. She feared for Pete as she read on. For rural communities shopping was a social activity and they still purchased their foodstuffs daily to ensure their freshness (not that word again), and also as a means of social engagement in community life. Yet that didn't seem to have perturbed him, for he'd merely scrawled 'notes for marketing' across the end of the article.

Then interview notes with farm suppliers, who were more keen to develop in other areas where the cash cow of Europe promised a more lucrative return. And market gardeners, it seemed, preferred to consider further expansion in fruit and flowers.

To the feasibility study. At last, she thought, and on reading it she was cheered again. For while it had swallowed most of Pete's own savings, it had also thankfully given him the green light, was confident that the market was there, if skilfully tapped, and made several practical suggestions as to how he might do so: start with the high-selling vegetables, market heavily on the approach of the winter months, emphasise the 'fresh' and 'nutritious' facets of his product, and keep his cost base as low as possible.

'Hi.' Pete stood in the doorway, a pizza in one hand and a six-pack in the other, grey eyes tired, his white skin stark and freckled beneath damp red hair.

'Great.' The flat box felt warm in her hands. Their fingers touched, and once he grinned, all doubts she'd harboured about his project eased. 'Tomato and cheese? Fab. And beer? Great. The opener's in the drawer.' She lifted a slice from the box and long strands of soft cheese hung from it as she took a bite, and she saw froth bubble up as Pete swooped beer into his mouth. 'Sit down. How did the meeting go?' she asked, mouth full of cheese.

'Good and bad, you know bank managers. Beer for you too?'

'Yeah, thanks. Give me the bad news first.'

'Can't get near the few pence my father left me until I'm twenty-five.' The beer made a white foam moustache on his upper lip. 'No, he won't yield on that, not a day before.'

'Damn.'

'And the good news ... great roll of drums ... he's finally confirmed that once I get the lump sum I can do as I please with it. Followed by the usual sermon. "It was your late father's wish that these monies be used to purchase a house, a home." Anyway, he's softened a bit, wants me to succeed, but only for my unfortunate father's sake, so he'll back me with a bank loan subject to an adequate feasibility study and business plan. Kiss me; I need to celebrate after that.'

'Don't. Your father would turn in his grave. Anyway, the government grants may come up trumps sooner ...'

'Can't count on that either,' he whispered, hands in her

hair. 'Multinationals and inward investment are all the rage, not much interest in us locals, poor souls. All I can count on for certain is you. Can I always do that?'

'I believe in you,' she said fiercely. 'Follow that dream; I just know that you'll succeed.' He was suddenly vulnerable, for she alone knew the hidden and frightened part of him so far removed from the bravado he presented to the captains and the kings of their newly industrialised world. 'Have more pizza first. I'm still hungry, aren't you?'

'Gave me other advice though too,' he continued. 'Suggested that for the first two years, I pare back as much as possible on my drawings.'

'How might you do that?'

'Well, rent's the heftiest one. We could ...' He glanced around.

'No,' she said firmly. 'You know I can't. I work in a Catholic hospital and you know what that means. We might though, we could marry sooner than planned, then nobody could object if you moved in then.'

He fell to his knees. 'Marry me. All my worldly goods I thee endow, my bike and my bus pass, the bank won't have them. How about that? And while you decide, I'll pour me another beer.'

'What if I say yes? I don't need the big spend.'

'A diamond engagement ring, one hundred to dinner, a foreign honeymoon?'

'I don't want most of that; a quiet wedding would suit me just fine. Yes, we *could* marry sooner,' she spoke slowly, 'then live here together. That'd save money.'

'Rose, I'm not willing to deprive you of your loveliest day. Forget it.'

'But what if I don't much want all that fuss? No, you

have the rest of the pizza, I've had enough.'

'Sure, thanks. Come on, every girl dreams of that.'

'Not true. All that dressing-up and display, well, it's not really me. I never once dreamt of a pavlova wedding gown, a net veil and a diamond tiara, more about having an interesting career.'

'Even a quiet wedding would cost too much.'

'We could cut it to a minimum.' Her voice grew more excited as she spoke. 'Then you move in here and we both live on my income until the business succeeds.'

'Why don't I just move in without all that? I'd pay my way, that would save a bit, and better still, we'd be together each night.'

'No,' she said firmly. 'No.'

'Why can't you be modern in that way, Miss Career Woman?'

'Because, well, I told you. And what's more, I believe sex is for marriage. I need a full commitment first.'

'I've already given you that. See, you don't fully trust me, want God on your side as well. Just like Dylan's masters of war? Is that it?'

'Are you suddenly against marriage?' she asked angrily. 'Know that if you ever move in, all housework is shared, and you just better be sure that you're modern enough to believe in that.'

'OK, OK, simmer down, I will tidy up. Don't you think we're still a bit young for something as awesome as a life's commitment?'

'But not too young to borrow vast sums of money?'

'Vast?'

'Well, vast to me.'

'Look, stop comparing it to salaries and wages, start any

business and the capital outlay is hefty'. He lowered his eyes as if ashamed he'd so little to offer her and she immediately softened. How she loved that unsure part of him that was visible only to her behind the hermitically sealed door of her flat and his heart. 'Look, the financial risks worry me too,' he conceded at last, 'I bet deep down you'd prefer I spend it on a house.'

'I believe in you, honest. And as I want to be honest with you too, yes, I want us to marry, the house can wait …'

'And I want us to have a proper marriage, but I can't afford it yet.'

'What makes it proper? The commitment we make to each other, our solemn vows. The rest, well, we can take or leave the rest. And yes, it will be sacred, I insist on that, with two witnesses present and before a priest.'

'My wife Rose,' he mused, 'hmm, what if I like the sound of that?'

'My husband Pete,' she smiled, suddenly shy, 'I'd like to be able to call you that.'

'Alright, we do it. And now that we've agreed to marry we can make love.'

'Must buy you a ring,' he agreed the following weekend.

They made their way by bus into the city and walked down O'Connell Street. 'Look, there's a jeweller, The Happy Ring House, we could try there.'

'We'll look in the window first.' It displayed three rows of wedding rings, gold bands that nestled in red velvet. 'What do you think?'

'Don't know, what's the difference between nine and eighteen carat gold?'

'Eighteen is more pure gold.'

'I'd like a plain band, not too wide, as my fingers,' she spread them before her, 'are quite small.'

'Come on, we'll go inside.'

They held hands as they stood at the glass-top counter and waited. 'We'd like to buy a wedding ring.'

'Of course sir, madam, we have a private room where you can peruse our selection.'

'No, no, here is fine,' said Rose hurriedly, fearful that that would cost money too.

'Then I shall measure your finger. And sir, do you plan to purchase too? Male wedding rings are fashionable now, we have an extensive line.'

'Oh Pete's not at all into fashion,' said Rose hurriedly, 'and neither am I. A narrow band, in gold, just for me.'

The long silver stick rattled with innumerable circles as he deftly selected one and put it on her third finger. 'Slightly large. Try this, two sizes up. Yes, I think so. Wait one moment please.'

'We saw one in the window we liked,' Rose called after him hurriedly, 'on the red velvet card, second row, third from left.'

'I think not,' he said as he set the card before her. 'Your hand is quite long, you see; this size is made to suit a short, plump one, so to speak. Try this.' He handed a ring to Pete and Rose blushed as he put it on. 'Nice,' he smiled. 'I shall get you a hand mirror.'

'Take your time, try a few more,' counselled Pete. 'Can't change it after, and it's meant to last.'

She spread her hand on the glass counter top and admired it, then held it up to the mirror and admired it again. 'I like this one.'

'You're sure?'

'Think so.'

'Walk around with it for half an hour or so,' said the jeweller generously, 'while you make up your mind.'

They did. She wore it nervously as they walked up the street as far as the Gresham together, then down past Clery's clock and back again. At times she placed her hand on his dark sweater and saw it glisten gold against it, at other times she spread her left hand out before her and admired it again.

'We'll take it,' they nodded.

Rose watched it being placed in a bed of ruffled blue silk and then the blue velvet box being firmly closed, as Pete searched in his pocket for notes.

'And with our compliments, a small snipe of champagne to celebrate.' Strong wires secured the cork of the bubbly over golden wrapping.

'Thanks,' they smiled as they left hand in hand.

Grace, as bridesmaid, immediately grew excited as to what Rose might wear, and insisted they trawl the shops – Arnotts, Brown Thomas, Switzers – to find a suitable dress. She went from shop rail to rail while a shivering Rose waited behind the closed curtain of a changing cubicle and tried them on. 'This. I think. Come out and let me see.'

'Grace, simmer down, you don't even believe in the marriage state.'

'True. I have a sense of occasion, though. No. Lovely, but not right for you. Try this one.'

'I like it, but it's far too expensive.'

'Oh damn the cost. You may just want an ordinary dress, but it is for your wedding day.'

'Look, we're doing it this way 'cause we don't have a bean between us. So I want a dress I might wear again.'

'Rose, you've got to dazzle for this one day, to hell as to whether it'll wash.'

'Get help. Pete's happy to marry me in jeans.'

She eventually decided on a knee-length crepe, in soft cream with a scooped-out neckline and tight sleeves, a colour that highlighted her hazel eyes, and a style that suited her unaffected nature.

'Your hair?'

'I'll wash it.'

'Now I'd style it this way, with a band of spring flowers to the back, I think. Shoes, let me think ... low heel, sling back, and we've got to find an exact match in colour. Who's best man?'

'Joe. You know, you've met him, Pete's pal from college. For the record, they'll both wear suits. What about you? Try and remember it's a "come as you are" wedding, with bride, groom, two witnesses, no more.'

'With cream? Let me think. Something muted. It's your day, mustn't outshine the bride, and all that. Turquoise, maybe, and you could tell Joe to have a tie and kerchief to match.'

'Outshine away, Grace. Just didn't know you fancied Joe.'

'Oh not Joe, not for me. Could wear cream too, I suppose, or maybe floral, given it's almost summer. What would you think of this? Don't ask about the price tag, I'll pay. And by the way, what do you two want for a gift. Decide, this is my first time as bridesmaid and I want to get something you'd really treasure, no vouchers or cheques.'

'We need a pressure cooker.'

'Rose, for pity's sake, when you only marry once.'

'We need one, for the winter, don't have central heating. I intend to continue working, and it'd cook a hot and tasty stew in twenty minutes.'

'Yes, I'll take this, come on, we'll go and get shoes, and then I'll treat you to lunch.'

Rose began the long, slow walk from the church doorway and up the aisle, nervous of the sound her heels made on its ancient wooden floor. She cast her eyes downwards to the bouquet of blood thorn blossoms Pete had sent, conscious that Grace, who followed, willed her to walk ever so slowly. The aisle stretched long and narrow ahead, and yes, Pete was there, she could see his broad back, straight in his new dark suit, a white circle of collar visible above it. Slowly still, past the Madonna's shrine that reminded her of the black queen she'd seen at Monserrat, the ancient goddess, now Christian mother, who had been born of woman, had mated and had birthed. A young schoolgirl paused to smile Rose's way then tip-toed with a lighted candle to the shrine. Slower still, her hands damp with nerves as they clutched her bouquet, past the shrine of Valentine bedecked with red roses. Their modern secular saint, once jailed for marrying lovers in breach of an emperor's edict that a young man's first duty must always be to his nation's wars. Nearer now, past the aged woman who touched her shoulder and wished her well, and close by the shrine of the saint of the Roses for whom she'd been named, by the French folk hero, the little flower, Saint Teresa.

'You are beautiful,' Pete smiled, and took her hand as the padre led their exchange of vows.

I, Rose Ann, she began as her turn came, voice clear in the silent church, *take you, Peter James, to be my lawful wedded husband*. The future stretched before her as some great unknown, *to have and to hold from this day forward*, and henceforth they would face it together, *For better, for worse; for richer, for poorer; in sickness and in health; 'til death us do part*. She shuddered at the enormity of the vow, and for a swift second wanted to race from the place, then felt almost heroic as she stayed to feel Pete squeeze her hand as he slid the narrow gold band down her third finger, over her second knuckle, to settle comfortably there. She felt the silver florin he placed on her open palm, saw him blush, ashamed he had so little of material wealth, as he closed her fingers over it to *all my worldly goods I thee endow*. Two altar boys carried the giant leather-bound register to a nearby table where she signed *Rose Ann Leahy*, then dated the event for 30th April, May Eve. Now wife, now wed.

They left the church to find it had rained outside, and they made their way by damp pavements across Grafton Street to Davy Byrne's. A giant platter, piled high with steaming oysters, awaited them there. Rose and Pete took the first two shells and prized them open; they placed an oyster on each other's tongues, and Rose tasted the salty and succulent flavour as it slipped down her throat. With brown bread, crusty and still warm from the oven. And Guinness, cream-topped and silky smooth.

'Speech. Speech,' joked Joe as he lifted his glass.

'Rose'll give a speech,' agreed Pete.

'Alright, I will,' said Rose, to everyone's surprise. 'First,' she began, 'I want to thank Grace and Joe for witnessing our vows, and thank them too for their wedding gifts. Thanks, Grace, for the magnificent Waterford crystal table piece (even if we still need saucepans), and thanks Joe too for your more than generous cheque. And Pete, who believes "loving is doing", most of all, my eternal thanks to you.'

'Pete. Pete. Speech from Pete,' cried Grace as they clapped and laughed.

Pete nodded. 'Rose and I dream dreams,' he began, 'very different dreams. As you know, my wife,' he glanced her way and smiled as he called her that, 'is aware of the great advances in pharmacy and she wishes to be part of bringing their healing to a wider public. I want to be my own boss, be part of the modernisation of agriculture and, what's more, I hope in time to create work for others as well as myself. And so today we have vowed to support each other in becoming more fully ourselves in these ways.'

'And,' Grace whipped a box from beneath the table, 'guess what? I brought a cake. Home-made, by *moi*. Iced white and decorated with small rings and hearts.'

'Oh Grace, you shouldn't have.' They cut through the hard icing to the dark mixture that fell away to almond icing then heavy fruit and nuts. 'First slice for the bride.'

'And champagne.'

'Joe! We didn't plan for any of this.'

'A toast.'

'Yes, a toast. To Rose and Pete. To Pete and Rose.'

'To Grace and Joe. To Joe and Grace.'

'Joe's asked me to sing.'

'Do sing, Grace, do.'

'You'll sing Grace, won't you?'

'Of course I'll sing. Let me think ... *This is my lovely day.*'

Later that evening the honeymooners took the bus to

Wicklow and held hands in nervous and excited anticipation as they passed through the villages that dotted the coast – Killiney, Shankill, Bray, Greystones, Delgany, Kilcoole, Brittas, Avoca – until they finally disembarked and walked to the small guesthouse they had booked for four nights. The next day they strolled together along sandy beaches, collected shells, and paddled and swam in the waves before hiding in high sand dunes to make love yet again. On their second day they took a bus inland and climbed Djouce, stretched out on the mountain plateau between the hills that circled all around them, and made love once more, then left the two small stones they had brought to the summit at the pagan monument there. They hired a small motor boat for their third day, and travelled south along the indented coastline, the wide sea to their left, the hills rising above and all around them to their right. Before they departed they explored small village shops, where they selected a memento from the gifts on offer, a small print of a Wicklow seascape. Come evening they returned to Dublin to find their double bed had been delivered by Clery's. They dismantled Rose's single and assembled the new one in its place, tore the heavy cardboard from the base, stripped the thick plastic from the mattress and placed it upon it. The snow-white undersheet, the oversheet, followed by two cream blankets with a pink trim. They made love again before they unwrapped the pillows, then fell into dreamless sleep.

Rose woke next morning happy.

6

'Work?' Grace thought when Rose spoke of her and Pete's elaborate career plans. 'What's that to me? Pays the bills, no more. My main love is music now.' It was, as she continued as a member of the G&R, was hopeful when she auditioned for Maria in *West Side Story*, grew glum when she failed to win the star part, and agreed, only after considerable pressure, to settle for a role as one of Maria's friends. Yet her solo ambitions were fulfilled shortly after as the church soprano, being pregnant, left suddenly. Grace replaced her, and so rendered *Stille Nacht* to a packed church at midnight mass, *Pia Jesu* to mark Good Friday, and *Bring Flowers* for the May celebrations.

'You've been selected for testing, Miss Donovan.' The firm hand of her boss pressed unexpectedly on her shoulder.

'A test?'

'New computer. We need staff with maths skills, and the state insists we also include our female staff.'

'Sums? I was never much use at them.'

'You sing, I believe?'

'Yes.'

'Music and maths are languages, Miss Donovan, and close cousins at that. Report to the boardroom for assessment, 9 a.m. Monday next.'

Import-Export's new computer was a monstrously large machine, hidden within high, forbidden walls of grey steel. It was rectangular in shape, housed in its own special room where it almost reached the ceiling. Its demands were constant: an even and unwavering temperature, an unbroken supply of electricity, and given the cost of each restart, employees prepared to work in shifts around the clock. Older employees viewed the changed world it heralded with scepticism, the younger among them with curious excitement, and it was in this context that the selected and newly promoted Grace was sent to share an office with Andy Newman, as computer work colleague.

Andy was of stocky build, and boasted a thick head of unruly black hair through which he ran his left hand in frustration at those who viewed this newly arrived machine with anything other than adoration. When they voiced their cynical views – and they did so often – Andy's grey eyes flashed with concealed annoyance, an attitude he immediately attempted to mask with a wide and generous smile.

Deeney, the production manager, who most hated Andy and all he stood for, went so far as to suggest that his five o'clock shadow reminded him of Nixon, a comparison Andy took as a compliment, for he naively loved and trusted all things American and, though he'd never been to the US, peppered his speech with alien phrases such as 'hell', 'goddam', 'no kidding' and, most especially, 'go for it', 'get to' and 'move'. All these, a cause for secret ridicule to some, were but tendencies that Grace viewed with mild amusement, for as managers in a new section, whose work innovations were resented by many, they wisely clung together as a team.

In truth, unlike Grace, who valued her much increased pay cheque but little else of her promotion, Andy had demonstrated a love of all things mechanical from an early age, a fascination for gadgets and objects that began with his mother's egg whisk, graduated to the kitchen tray on which he hurled himself downhill through his first snowfall, to fast bikes and scooters, both of which he'd ridden, to larger and speedier cars for which he still yearned, and now Import-Export's first computer. Indeed, by this time Andy's tendency to view all of life through mechanical lenses extended to women, a group from which he managed, after some inner confusion, to exclude Grace, who, to him, was as some third sex: female, but, given her surprisingly speedy grasp of computer mechanics, could hardly be considered feminine.

Despite this, or perhaps because of it, they worked well together as a team in their recruitment drive for young people to staff the company's new computer centre.

'You quiz them for the personal skills, I'll look after the technical. OK?'

'Sure, Andy, I know we need team players,' she agreed as they perused CVs together, long-listed, short-listed, then called for assessment, interview, and finally for a group dynamic day.

The staff they sought initially were to code numerically, a task that involved the transfer of vast quantities of information from the production, marketing and financial sectors of the company onto red-lined rectangular columns, in a manner that required accuracy and, given the cost of the operation, speed. The coded information was then punched onto rectangular cardboard cards that Andy fed lovingly into the computer, as it purred calmly in gratitude for its constant feed. Occasionally, and without warning, it chose to gurgle, a sound akin to that of water as it disappeared down an ancient bath hole. The noise filled Grace with terror, but Andy responded in the soothing manner of romantic to distressed lover. It always obliged him in return with output: giant sheets of paper that carried vast amounts of information (previously acquired manually and over a far longer time span) for their respective company sectors. Andy coordinated the time use and fought endlessly with sector management on costs while Grace, as good cop, soothed ruffled feathers when errors or delays occurred. Once their own teams were in place and the new system was working smoothly, Grace relaxed, but not so Andy.

'Hell, guess what,

why not lease out our surplus time to clients?'

'Andy, take it easy, it's up and running smoothly at last and we both deserve a rest.'

'Go for it, Grace. There's money to be made on this one. I'll propose it at the next meeting. You'll back me, won't you?' He looked so boyishly eager as he talked in that way, and his wide smile softened her resistance, as did the promise of the hefty commissions that would follow. For Andy was never still, always pushing the boundaries. 'Hell, Grace, why don't we sell our experience to others? Gained a lot of tech knowledge here, could advise them on computer purchase, then recruit and train for them. I need you, I need you to back me with this, got to get it past Deeney who'll do his damnedest to block it. If you keep him with us, I can handle the others.'

'Andy, take a break, we both need one.'

'Goddam it, you still don't see the computer's enormous potential? And we've got to go for it. Sure there are still problems. The machines are still far too large, too expensive and heavy to transport, unwieldy too, and take up far too much space. Breakthrough on all those'll come, it has to. Read the most recent research I sent you? Most of all, it's got to be done cheap, and for mass production.'

'Get a life, Andy.'

'What do you mean? There's money to be made. Like billions.'

'I earn enough. So do you, for that matter.'

'Get to, Grace, no one gets to have a decent life without money. You'll back me, I know you will.'

'Hell Grace,' he said again sometime later. 'Just thought of something. Yeah, I think we just might pull this one off.'

'What's it this time? Look, the consultancies and trainings are fine, but I don't want any more work, and don't talk money to me, because I'm earning as much as I'll ever need now.'

'Those new computers, small as fridges, why don't we woo them?'

'Woo? Who?'

'The manufacturers. Get them here and make them in Ireland.'

'Andy, one thing is certain. You're not going to win this one.'

'I won't? Want to bet? Back me. I need you, got to get it past the management and board here first. Deeney will be troublesome as always, lazy dosser, won't shed his rural roots, bog cotton still growing out of his ears. Should have stayed shoaling fish and digging turf. He works a bit each spring, thinks he's still sowing seeds, wakes up again to reap a bit come autumn. Doesn't even believe in the eight-hour clock, let alone a twenty-four-hour cycle.'

'Come on, Andy, Deeney's like everyone's grandfather here.'

'Know what, Grace? Deeney's Ireland's dead. Soon our Dublin will be another New York, up there with the best of 'em as a city that never sleeps. And you can keep him in line. Don't know how you do it, you're a genius at that, for you can always stop him swinging key meetings his way. Just keep him with us, and I can handle the rest of 'em. Can't do anything much without our management and board's backing. But with them behind me ... and there'll be commissions ... how much do you want? Just name your price.'

Let's see, how will I do it up? Grace stood at the door of her new apartment and viewed the bare room beyond, then went impulsively to the low windows and held the rich brocade curtains to her cheek. How she loved that view, the night skies and the city lights reflected in the waters below. And the large grate, with a blazing log fire come winter. She didn't plan to use the central heating which was strangely cold by comparison, and she'd ordered her music into neat catalogues on the side shelves beside it: sacred arias, then the classics, followed by stage musicals, with the few pop groups, primarily her Beatles, all branded together.

And the computer books, how heavy they weighed as she transferred her growing library of journals and texts to the second bedroom, she'd furnish it as a study to be used when she brought work home. The main bedroom boasted wall-to-wall wardrobes, they'd contain her business suits, all cut in a similar style, pencil-slim skirt, silk top and neat jacket, which she'd soften with a matching necklet, or a lapel brooch. Indulged too was her weakness for shoes, for she now owned several dozen, their heels sufficiently high to enhance her authority as she stood shoulder to shoulder with Andy. And finally the kitchen, she'd stock it weekly with fresh fruit and vegetables from the stall holders on Moore Street who'd also ply her with newly plucked seasonal flowers and potted plants.

At that most special business dinner, Grace circled the table in search of her name place. She had prepared carefully for such a formal night, had her hair coloured and wore it loose in a manner that softened her efficient business expression, and had finally selected an elegant silk to wear, a dress that was simply cut, and in shades of orange and flame red that flattered her sallow skin. 'Grace Donovan'. With Deeney to her left, she sighed, as usual, and Chuck Wingfield, from the visiting delegation, to her right. She glanced across the table to Andy, who nodded curtly towards Deeney. Yes, she knew what he expected of her, Deeney's doom-laden eyes left her in no doubt of that. Their production manager was to be curtailed in his noisy yearnings for a simpler past; her night's task was to keep Deeney gagged.

The tables rose and applauded the guests of honour as they made their way through the lavish setting to the top of the room. Three government ministers known to Grace from TV, the American ambassador, two senior civil servants from Industry and Commerce, the head of the Industrial Development Authority, and several others she didn't recognise.

'Be seated.'

'Hi, I'm Grace. You're most welcome, Chuck.'

'Thanks. Say, can you tell me what's that your harpist plays?'

Grace listened for the soft string sounds that rose

beyond the din of noisy chatter and food being served. 'It's called *I Hear You Calling Me*. Our tenor John McCormack made it famous.'

'From some old black and white movie I once saw. Knew I heard it somewhere before.' Their table was served, a succulent starter of smoked salmon, dark pink against a bed of green salad leaves, its velvet flavour tangy with lemon juice, accompanied by a French dry white.

'Our Miss Donovan has a fine voice too,' interjected Deeney.

'Oh don't,' she retorted, embarrassed.

'Hell, I sing in the shower too,' offered Chuck with a large smiled that creased his tanned face, as he reached for the brown bread.

'So you like our harp?' continued Deeney. 'Are you in any way Irish?'

'One eighth,' Chuck nodded. 'Sullivan on my mother's side. Her forebears sailed from Castletownbere in 1872.' Grace smiled covetously to where Andy sat, aware that Chuck, despite his rural origins, exuded the sort of American confidence her colleague could never hope to emulate. Deeney moved to talk with the guest to his left, while Chuck called across the table to where Jos Eliot Jr sat. 'You going anywhere Saturday, Jos?'

'Fly back home over London.'

'Hell, stay an extra day.'

'I stay I miss the Red Sox match.'

'Stay, and we'll get you tickets for a hurling match,' offered Deeney.

'Yeah,' Chuck seemed keen, 'I've heard about that. You play it with ash sticks, fastest ball in the world, I'd enjoy seeing that.'

'Or you could do a castle tour,' offered Grace quickly. She leaned back in her chair as the main course arrived, rack of lamb served with mint sauce, petit pois, and new potatoes. 'See Dublin Castle, visit the castle at Malahide as well.'

'Nice to tell the folks back home I'd been to a castle,' Chuck mused. 'Planned to go down Cork way, hoped Jos would come with me.'

'Grace'll accompany you,' offered Deeney with a smug grin towards Andy. She glanced at him, surprised, but his expression remained innocent and gave no indication of the revenge that drove him.

'You will, Grace?' Chuck accepted a second serving of lamb, and his hand momentarily touched hers.

'Well, thank you,' she retorted lightly. The celebratory atmosphere of the room had made her giddy, and as she took another sip of wine she knew the drinks went straight to her head. A long weekend stretched ahead, and she had little planned for it, save a few non-essential domestic tasks. Why not? They could drive down early on Saturday and return Sunday night, pause at Cashel and again at Blarney Castle. Chuck would enjoy all that, then find his old homestead close by the wildly exotic Beara Peninsula.

Her life had been about work for far too long, why not celebrate for a change and have some fun? And yes, she would have dessert, a small helping of profiteroles, thickly covered with chocolate and served with whipped cream. Followed by a selection of cheeses, and coffees. She proffered her cup for a second helping when the room fell silent as the minister stood and called on the delegation head to speak. His voice came to her, backed by the stringed accompaniment of 'Galway Bay'.

' ... Yes, we have decided. We have chosen your beautiful country as the European base where we will manufacture our new, more compact computers.' The tables rose as one, to the loud pop of champagne corks and calls for a toast. The golden bubbles flowed into her glass, as she raised it high.

'It's thousands of jobs for your folk.'

Her glass clicked with Chuck's. 'Hey, and this is just the start of things.' She laughed as their eyes locked, then sipped and felt the liquid fizzle in her mouth, then catch against the back of her throat. She stretched her glass towards Andy, and found him staring straight across at her.

She looked in some way different to him, she'd done something to her hair that made it glow a deep auburn red, and her wide lips were softly parted as she sipped again, then laughed back up at Chuck. He watched as the American millionaire scanned the dress she wore appraisingly, saw him note that it revealed a slight hint of cleavage, watched him glance down her body and value how it narrowed to her waist then fell softly over her curved hips. What did this Chuck jerk mean to her anyway, and why did she behave as if this, all of this, was of his making, when he, Andy, had worked night and day to get their godforsaken country to this place. He had held faith, had believed, had never once doubted they could win this contract, and he'd done it despite the fiercest competition from abroad, coupled with untold mockery and doubts from home.

And here was Grace, who knew all that, behaving as if this newly arrived Yankee jerk, who'd merely flown in for a day, had achieved it all single-handed. What did she mean? His eyes blazed with jealous fury. Didn't she know, above all else, that SHE WAS HIS?

Grace woke to a mild hangover, her stomach was nauseous and she had a slight headache. When she opened her eyes it was apparent that she was in a strange room, and lying on a strange bed. Someone had just left it, for the covers beside her were thrown back and when she stretched out her hand to touch the mattress, she found it still warm beneath her palm. It was daytime too, for a long beam of light fell to the floor between the curtains, while the city sounds of cars, horns and brakes floated in from outside. Close by, the bedside locker boasted an empty champagne bottle, a wired cork thrown carelessly beside it, while beyond that, a long trail of discarded clothes led from the bed to the door. White male jocks beside her lace panties, his white shirt with her white bra, her flame dress and white slip atop a black dinner jacket and bow.

She pulled the sheet closer up her naked body then glanced to her left from where bathroom sounds competed with the traffic outside, the furious pelt of shower water against tiles, a vigorous scrubbing of teeth followed by loud gargling ... *I'll take you home again* ... and singing. He emerged from the bathroom drying his hair, a second white towel secured at his waist.

'Andy!' Droplets of water clung to the dark hair that matted his chest and fell to the floor as he laughed aloud.

'Can't shave.' He sat beside her on the bed and rubbed his chin ruefully. 'No razors here; supplies of soap, conditioner, shampoo, you name it, but no razor.' The bed creaked as he bent towards her. 'Hi.' He stroked her cheek lovingly. 'Guess what? We've got to do this more often.'

'I'm still half asleep.'

'Breakfast, then. What'll you have? Full Irish?'

'Christ, Andy.' She crawled out of bed, dragged the oversheet with her, and made her way to the bathroom.

'I'll order for you?'

'Coffee. Black. That'll do just fine.'

The mirror told her she was a mess, hair dishevelled, eyes bloodshot, with mascara smudges down her cheeks. Andy! Come Monday, they had to work together again, as if none of this had happened, and again on Tuesday, and for the many days that followed.

'That was quite a night,' he called after her.

'Coffee would be fine,' she repeated.

'You rest a bit,' he continued. 'I'm on my way out, got to collect my new car by ten. Be back by eleven, then drive you to your place. OK?'

'What car did you decide on?' she asked, glad to change the subject.

'BMW in the end. Decided you can't beat the Germans for motors, though the Japs are catching up fast.'

She waited 'til the bedroom door banged and then went to the window. She watched until he appeared below, saw him pause as the hotel porter summoned a taxi, that drove him away. It had rained softly during the night, the footpath below damp as the city stirred from sleep and shoppers in raincoats and with umbrellas made their way past. How foolish her dress felt now, how ridiculously high her shoes, and how tired she still felt, unbelievably tired and still in need of sleep.

'Hi, come down, can't wait for you to see it.' He wrapped her in the comforting warmth of his dinner jacket which she clutched to her, and held her hand as they made their way to the lift. The cream upholstery squeaked as she sat into the car.

'Nice,' she agreed, then glanced back to where the rear seat was still covered in cellophane.

'Want to collect anything on the way? Fresh milk, newly baked bread?'

'No, just want to get home, shower and change. I can get groceries later.'

'See you Monday then.' His lips glazed her cheek and his eyes held hers fondly. 'Oh, by the way,' he took a velvet box from the glove compartment, 'that's for you.'

Inside was a narrow necklet in spun gold.

'You shouldn't.'

'Put it on.'

'It's so beautiful.'

'Lovely on you. Now get some sleep, and see you again Monday.'

With his new-found wealth Andy built up a share portfolio in which he rejected the blue chip, dull but safe options of bank stock and 'buy to lease' property, and invested instead in high-risk oil (in Saint George's Channel and off north Mayo), anticipated an explosion in specialist software packages, and also backed a new factory that planned to manufacture medical devices in the Lee river basin. 'I've a gut for what'll succeed,' he explained to Grace when she urged him to exercise greater caution, 'just follow that.'

He bought a home too, a large mansion in Killiney, the property of a deceased First World War widow, a nineteenth-century tumbledown affair that boasted turrets, for in a previous life it had had pretensions of being a castle. His new neighbours included a pop singer, a film director (he was separated from them both by an avenue of ancient trees that howled like a banshee in the wind) and the residence of the ambassador of some obscure Arab state of which he'd never heard.

Despite endless efforts by his friendly builder, his new floor-length windows still rattled, his newly installed central heating rumbled and gurgled with no warning at odd hours of the day and night, and after no less than three failed efforts to fully seal the door frames, slight drafts made his new curtains waft back and forth in an eerie and ghost-like manner at unexpected times. And despite his installation of a vastly expensive new plumbing system, and no less than three ensuites, Andy just had to resign to a shower that did little more than dribble, for the pressure required for an all-powerful American blast just wasn't there.

And while waiting for his new home to be completed, Andy joined the requisite clubs: Portmarnock (though he didn't play golf), Fitzwilliam (where his best efforts were at a modest game of squash), and the National Sailing (but only after the Royal George had refused him), where his bright suggestion that the sailing frat diversify into water skiing and speed boats, in the interest of livening things up, met with a stony response, and he seldom sailed after that.

He went on to join the RDS, nearer his city workplace, but on his first attendance at the Horse Show unexpectedly found he was not amidst the beautiful people but rather jammed within an influx of farmers who obsessed on the price of heifers and the current yields on milk. Showjumping proved boring, and, eager to engage more actively with the nags, he applied for membership of the Phoenix Park polo, but as ownership of one's own horse was de rigueur and as his new home, alas, didn't have stables, he missed out there. Over several months of winter Saturdays he made his way to various southside rugby grounds in the biting cold and there learnt to appreciate the passion and rivalry of the club game in the capital. Grace occasionally accompanied him on these social adventures (at least to those that included women) and found them accepted as a couple. He took delight to find their photos in the social columns of the Sundays, in *Social and Personal*, and in the *Irish Tatler*, and welcomed the comments on Grace, who happily was not described as pretty (too dolly) or elegant (too old) but by the supreme accolade of 'attractive'.

'You could join a charity committee or two, Grace, meet the right people. It's all who you know and where to be seen. I might have been accepted by the Royal George if you'd known Reginald's wife on ...'

'And take the raw look off our greed?'

'Hell, go for it, Grace. Be a pal, and join the charity molls for a bit, make a few new friends there, toss it around among them that we're a pair.'

'Not for me, Andy, can't somehow get my head around sipping champagne and downing smoked salmon in the interests of alleviating poverty.'

Yet she continued to entertain clients with him, sometimes at the Shelbourne, preceeded by aperitifs at the Horseshoe bar, on other occasions at the Mirabeau in Sandycove, and in winter evenings at the Guinea Pig in Dalkey as the latter boasted real coal fires, built from turf, which always impressed American guests. Increasingly, Grace had many acquaintances but few friends, but she seldom noticed, for the installation of the smaller computers spelt ever more recruitment and staff training, advice meetings with clients, and consultancies with other companies.

'Look, we've got to stay one step ahead of the rest, that's how this computer world works.'

'Simmer down, Andy, I will back you at Tuesday's meeting, OK?'

'Hell, Grace, there are so few software packages as yet, got to convince them it's an area absolutely ripe for expansion.'

'Just don't push it too hard, give them time for it to sink in.'

'You think I'm too pushy?'

'With me? No, I'd never accuse you of that.' She smiled, for in truth they made love infrequently, as it became an event that marked a part of their business life, a late-night celebration that came with yet another successful deal, after the staff Christmas party, or on his return from a long trip away. Lovemaking was an event he usually followed with an expensive gift – a piece of jewellery, a bracelet, a brooch, earrings, none of which she much wore. Yes Grace liked Andy, knew she always had, was comfortable and at ease with the familiarity he offered. He occasionally and fleetingly mentioned marriage, and when she shook her head he quickly nodded in agreement, there was time enough for that in four, five years' time; he was in no rush either.

And so her social life continued to revolve almost totally around business lunches, marketing dinners, a life lived increasingly in a successful cocoon with a bubble of like-minded folks. Yet she did stay in touch with Rose, now the one contact she retained outside that tight circle, despite the fact that Rose alone of those she now knew challenged the cosy consensus that now was her life.

'If Andy's that good to you, I wouldn't string him along like that.'

'Oh come on, the situation suits both of us just fine.'

'The shift to computers is a bit of a nightmare where I work. Nurses are still trained to record everything in notebooks, while consultants cling to their paper charts, and it's they who call the shots. We've now got three record systems running: notebooks as they've been around since Florrie's day; charts, beloved of the consultants and they won't part with them; and now the new screen as well. Trouble is, each transcription increases the risk of error.'

'But think of the storage advantages, goodbye to archives of paper records, and immediate access to all information.'

'Errors are serious, can even mark the difference between life and death.'

Yet despite their disagreements, and the fact that Pete disliked Andy, they remained friends.

'Does he have to treat Pete as just another customer?'

'Everyone's that to Andy, Rose.'

'Come on, he might take time off now and then. He behaves as if they both reside on some fantasy ladder, with Andy always on the higher rung. While Pete's about food, knows that with all the computers in the world we all still got to eat.'

'Pete's stuck in the past, we've done precious little else since the Famine save produce and export food.'

'Well, I'm with Pete, and I work at the coalface of who lives and who dies.'

'Come on, we're not going to compete and disagree like our men.'

'Right on, for sooner or later you'll meet someone else anyway.'

'I've met someone else.' Grace broke the news to Andy in the computer room as the steel giant purred on beside them. She had purposely chosen to inform him there, for she feared a replay of that evening when they had first ended up in bed. Andy was like that, took her for granted most of the time, and then grew masterful if she showed any signs of finding another. Here, in a room forbidden to most staff, they could be private, but not completely so. She watched carefully for his reaction as she spoke, saw him slowly put aside the giant printout he'd held, then run his hand through his thick locks and look at her in amazement. 'I'm sorry, Andy.'

'You're telling me we're through?'

'Don't raise your voice.' She glanced nervously towards the door. 'Look,' she continued sotto voce, 'we've been great work colleagues and the best of friends, I'm grateful for that, always will be.'

'Grateful!' he shouted. 'We were to marry.'

'Were we? Andy, don't shout, you want the whole office to hear? OK, we made love occasionally.'

'Be together for life, for fifty, for sixty years.'

'I never wanted marriage or children.'

'Sure, not straight away. And neither did I, but in five, seven years' time. I wasn't in much of a rush either, it suited us both to wait.'

'Andy, I've thought a fair bit about this. Over the last week or two. You don't want me much; it's more that you don't want anyone else to have me.' His expression told her that she had hit home for he paled, then steadied himself against the computer. 'You're married to your job, probably always will be. And you like the computer parts of me, managerial, organised, competent and efficient. There are other parts of my life that matter a lot to me, and you still don't even know that they exist.'

'So you've fallen in love?' His voice grew mocking. 'For the very first time, I suspect? With who? With fucking who?'

'No one you know or will ever know.' His eyes grew menacing and for the first time she feared him. 'Look,' she said, 'always know that I'm so truly grateful for the last years, always will be.'

'And now it's over, just like that.'

'Andy, please don't take it this way. We can still work together, remain friends too if you want.'

'Fuck friendship, you conniving bitch. You made a high-powered career here because of me. Me! Without me you'd never have got beyond the typing pool, without me you were going fucking nowhere. Fuck, fuck you.'

'Not true. Now, if you'd please excuse me.'

She was determined to retain her career, though in the days that followed, the tension between them grew almost unbearable, but she developed an icy defence and a cool determination not to blink firs. Three weeks later, Andy suddenly left. Without warning, for she arrived at work one Monday to find his side of their office stripped and the workplace abuzz with gossip, that he'd been headhunted and made an offer he couldn't refuse, in New Zealand; and Grace would now manage the computer section, with a soon-to-be-recruited manager who would be junior to her. Grace was in love again, and determined not to see beyond that state. Only Rose knew the whole truth of her past. Rose, who wondered if she might contact Andy, lonely and alone at the other side of the globe, phone him, even write? In the end Rose did none of these things, but come Christmas she sent him a card that wished him peace. Some months later she bumped into one of his friends, who told her he'd returned to Ireland once, to attend as best man at a younger brother's wedding. With a new partner? No. Unaccompanied. She heard nothing further of him after that.

7

Rose sat on the bus home, hugged the secret to herself and smiled quietly. She'd told no one as yet, not even Pete, for she'd first believed the nausea was the result of something she'd eaten, and it wasn't until she'd realised her period was late that she'd suspected. She took the note from her bag, opened the white page and read it again: 'Pregnancy test result: Positive.' Just when had it happened, when had that speediest of sperms penetrated her one ovum as it made its leisurely way downwards to meet it? Two weeks back from ... when had her last period been due ... yes, that was the most likely time. That weekend, on the Friday evening when they'd first gone to hear The Dubliners. Luke Kelly had sung 'Raglan Road', then 'The Black Velvet Band' and 'The Wild Rover', and on their way home they'd pulled in to the layby at Sandymount strand for they just couldn't wait, had made love urgently as the waves lapped outside and the moon cast a long road of light on the sea before them. Had it been then?

Two stops more, she was almost home, but she wanted to be certain to tell Pete. Or perhaps it had been the following night when they'd made love again, on the old sofa, as Gay Byrne had interviewed Ustinov on TV and later Phil Lynott had chatted with him about a rock version of 'Whiskey in the Jar'. Or maybe it had been the following Monday when Pete had come home saying he'd sealed that deal, that large supermarket chain who'd finally agreed to give him shelf space, and so they'd forgotten about dinner and gone straight up to bed instead. She yearned to know, but could never be certain, yet still wanted it to be a time they might always remember together .

'Sit down.' Pete patted the sofa, then wrapped a rug around her. 'Now, what can I get you?'

'I'm not ill,' she chided, yet smiled and lay back on the couch, contented.

'Might at least go out and buy us a snipe of champagne to celebrate.'

'Can't drink.' She took his hand and placed it on her belly. 'It's still underage.'

'You've made me the happiest man,' he whispered, and she felt his fingers softly stroke her cheek.

'Dad,' she grinned, 'how will it feel to have someone call you that?'

'I'll take it very seriously,' he nodded, 'and do solemnly vow to be a good father, to protect and provide.' She sensed his pleasure that he could now confidently do that, for his business was profitable and he made monthly savings towards a deposit on their first house. 'Did the doc give you a due date?'

'Twenty-fifth of July. Wanted to know if you'd attend.'

'If *you* want me there.'

'Sure I want you present.' She patted her belly again. 'This is *our* child. The midwife thinks better not, says that men are clueless around birth, look on all helpless then are disappointed that the firstborn hasn't arrived as a two-year-old all togged out for football. Says the truth is that you're the fragile sex, abysmal cowards before life's greatest mystery.'

'I said I'll be there if you want.'

'She even went on to say that new infants are very demanding, and that they roar endlessly for food for the first six weeks. *Nessun Dorma* time she called it, when none shall sleep. Said men aren't much use then either when they don't have what's very best for baby, breast milk. Not married, what would she know anyway? I'm just so thrilled, so excited. Aren't you?'

'I'm your new man, will be there. Now you and I have still got to eat, so what'll you have? I'll cook.'

'Tea and toast is fine, I've already had a meal at work. You have a beer, go on, I know you'd love one.' She watched him plug in the kettle, drop two slices into the toaster, then pour a beer and raise the glass towards her. 'Here's to us soon to be three. Tea's up in a minute.'

'With two sugars.' The white foam moustache that the beer left on his upper lip made her smile. 'I can't think of a baby as "it",' she confided as she drank. 'Can we agree on a name even if we're to change it later? A boy's name, for I know you want a son, all men want that.'

'I want all this to go well, and you both to be healthy. A name? Rose, of course, if it's a girl.'

'Thanks, but no, far too confusing.'

'Roisin then, for "little Rose".'

'Not keen on that.' She bit into the toast. 'Say it's a boy and think of a name for him.'

'Can't think of one right now.'

'OK, start by a process of elimination. What don't you like?'

Well, nothing too long. You want more toast? Leahy's two syllables, and Pete and Rose are short names. And something Irish, so nothing like William or George, or Samantha or Victoria for a girl.'

'Samantha or Victoria? Have another beer if you want.'

'They'd just be shortened anyway to Sam or Vick and I'd

hate that. 'I want "it" to be called by the name we give "it", not Teresa shortened to Tee or Maureen to Mo.'

'Start at the beginning of the alphabet then.'

'Abigail-Abraham, until we know the sex. Ab-Abe for short.'

'Be serious. Look, I'm just not calling it "it" for nine months, or "the bump", which is even worse.' She sensed he wanted to hug her but was suddenly nervous that sex might hurt her or damage the baby. 'It's fine, honest, I asked the doc. Sex life to continue as normal.'

'You're sure?'

'Yeah, and I want to celebrate with more than just a mug of tea.'

'Great. To bed then, wife, to bed.'

'I'm here.' Grace burst into the flat, full of static energy that blazed across Rose's quiet joy. 'Where's the new da, must congratulate him too.'

'Pete's working, he'll be home in an hour or so.'

'Show me, how d'you look, no bump yet?'

'It's not a bump, its Ab-Abe until we find a name we can agree on farther down the alphabet.'

'What?'

'Abigail-Abraham.'

'Get it. Names can only improve after that. I'm godmother, I presume. I'd enjoy that. And to celebrate I'll have a drink, even if you're limited to barley water. Where are they? Only beer? That'll do for now, I suppose. Well, here's to the next generation. Do I want to feel that old? No, but, here's to the three of you.'

'Thanks. Sit down and chat for a bit. Doc says we're healthy, expects everything to go just fine.'

'So what else is there to say about pregnancy and all that? And I know you're just dying to know who my new love is. Well, we're still going strong, ever since I had that "this is it" feeling, knew he was my Mr Perfect right from the very start. You may even know him already,' she smiled coyly. 'And you know what's wonderful about being in love again? Well, when I remember back now and recall those past loves, I remember them all as just the greatest guys. Juan, remember him? So sweet, and we were both so young, came all the way from Spain just to claim me. Imagine I was loved that much and I only nineteen.'

'You hardly remember Father Y in that way?'

'Oh but I do, and you won't believe this, but he's been promoted. I couldn't believe it when I read it. And once I heard it I knew I'd just have to have a look. See how he was too. Got my hair done specially for the occasion, couldn't have him forget what a turn-on my glorious locks had once been for him.

So I sallied forth to Saturday evening mass – *Kyrie Eleison*, *Christe Eleison* – arrived a bit late and slipped into a rear pew. I could see the altar clearly, and guess what? He looked cute as ever, a small line of pale skin naked and bare just above the nape of his neck. And his hands. He raised them to bless us all. God, how I remember those hands. *Kyrie Eleison*. Being so happy myself I just wanted to thank him, you know, for … well, for as it was in the beginning, for what once had been very good times.'

'How's work?' asked Rose quickly as she glanced towards the door. Pete, she expected, would return soon, and they'd planned to spend a quiet evening together.

'I've eased off a fair bit at work,' Grace confessed. 'It's quieter there now, without Andy driving everyone at an

American rate of knots. Did him a favour. You know it's true, don't look at me like that, I'm sure New Zealand suits Andy just fine. You'll be pleased to hear that I've finally given away all that jewellery he gave me.'

'Good idea, unless you planned to build up a collection on a par with Mrs Simpson or Liz Taylor after her fifth husband. What'd you do with it?'

'Wrote first, to his workplace, and asked for an address as initially I thought of returning it to him. No reply. Then wrote again and asked if he'd prefer if I gave it to charity, but got no reply to that either. So eventually gave it all to the VdeP and wrote and told him I'd done that. Failed to answer that letter too. The old fellow in their charity office seemed a bit taken aback, asked me to sign that it hadn't been "acquired illicitly". How could he possibly have thought that of me? Anyway, can I have another beer?'

'Sure. You want something to eat too?'

'No, not hungry. You have something?'

'No, I'm just fine.'

'I think I know a fair bit about men by now, Rose, and you know, that's the nicest feeling. They're different from us, and guess what? That's what makes them so exciting. I mean I'd never be much switched on by a male with long flowing locks now, would you?

'Of the four men I've had, each one wanted a different part of me, you know? I mean, to Juan I'll always be *hermosa Irlandés*, his green goddess, virginal, pure and young. And to Y, his mighty saint-whore, his Magdalene, hair locks dipped low over his God almighty crotch. Andy, surprise, surprise, was drawn to my brain, helped him win all those megabuck business deals, not that I ever got as much as an ounce of credit for any of that in their boring old annual reports. And I'm in love again, at last. No, I'm not telling you anymore, but I promise we'll all get together soon. And what matters too is that I'm singing as I never sang before.'

'G&R already rehearsing for their winter season? What show is it this time?'

'*The King and I*. And I so, so wanted the lead.'

'As usual. Oh come on, Grace, Anna isn't you. "Hello, Young Lovers" is for geriatrics who've thrown in the towel, you don't sound ready for that yet by a long shot.'

'The main plot, as I read it, is about how Anna tries to explain romantic passion, Western style, to the Asian ruler, when he hadn't a bog about it, poor shit. She tries so hard to get him to understand that "across a crowded room" grand moment; the tragedy is he just doesn't get it, refuses to separate his virility from his fertility and clings on to the belief that it's all about having hordes of kids. Anyway, I kicked up such a rumpus when they failed to cast me as Anna that they threw me on the list for audition for Tuptim, the slave girl.'

'And how did that go?'

'Surprise, surprise, I found it was somehow truly me, and that I could sing "I Have Dreamed", with all my heart and soul somehow in it. At the audition everyone around me suddenly went silent. Not just the cast and chorus, but the make-up artists and the technicians as well; when I'd finished you could hear a pin drop. No one said anything for a minute and I felt a bit frightened, then the applause began, and they clapped and clapped and clapped. The casting director then asked for "We Kiss in the Shadows" and I just knew I'd found my role. Got the two best songs in the show this season, two marvellous showstoppers.

You'll come to the opening night, want you there in the front row. Let me know in advance if you want a ticket for Pete as well.'

'You're happy to play a slave girl who yearns to be free?'

'She's the showstopper, and that's what counts with me.'

Over the weeks that followed, Rose's excitement diminished as she grew drained from the morning sickness, embarrassed at the frequency that had her rush endlessly to the bathroom, and heavy with tiredness, a weary exhaustion such as she'd never experienced before. And while her belly still remained flat, her breasts grew swollen and ached, while the endless standing that her work demanded made her feet ache too. three a.m., awake again and hungry, she craved, yes, an onion sandwich, yes, with salt, pickles, vinegar and black olives. How could Pete suggest an early breakfast with scrambled eggs and sizzling rashers, how that smell repelled, almost as bad as percolated coffee that she suddenly couldn't stand.

The clinic midwife seemed unperturbed at all this as she ticked boxes: no cigarettes, no alcohol, no medically prescribed drugs, right age, right weight, right size, normal pregnancy and delivery expected, everything fine. Rose flicked through a magazine as she awaited the obstetrician, viewed those who waited with her with a new curiosity — young girl, no more than seventeen, fingers ringless, who quietly wept, stern mother close by who suddenly crumpled and wept silently too; an older woman, hair already white, her face frozen in a 'still startled to find myself pregnant' expression; another her own age, her belly enormous, who made Rose wonder in alarm if she might swell to such a giant size also. Doctor then, who prodded her belly, ticked further boxes and pronounced her fine too. She first felt 'it' (the bump, now Paul if a boy, Ann if a girl) move inside her some weeks later. Yes, it had done that, fluttered somewhere between her waistband and her navel, and as her left palm moved to her belly she felt it again, in surprised amazement. Yes, her baby had actually moved.

'How beautiful you look.' Pete's hand lay on her belly as he waited for the foetus to move again.

'Me?' she asked, surprised.

'Yes, you.'

'Well, thanks,' she grinned.

She left work with the gifts she'd received at her baby shower, a silver photo frame from the pharmacists, a soft wool blanket from the nurses who knew her best, a hand-knitted cardigan from the cleaning lady, a cheque from the interns, with several cards signed with messages of goodwill. She spent the cheque on a Moses basket, placed it in the sunny spare room, the wool blanket and cardigan atop, and then positioned the empty photo frame on the small shelf above it. Then she packed her hospital case in anticipation – Sudocrem, Vaseline, nappies, tiny vests and babygros for the baby, with a dressing gown, night dresses and underwear for herself. Then, one afternoon, when the sun coaxed her outside, she impulsively went to the shops and bought toys – a symphony of bells that waved softly as the door opened and tinkled, a colourful mobile of bright butterflies and a cuddly brown teddy bear. And then, fully prepared, she settled down one afternoon to read again *A History of Baby and Child Care*. Of Truby King, godfather of the Victorian nursery, he who'd taught Her Majesty the

Queen's loyal subjects that cleanliness was next to godliness, that mothers were the angels of the house, of a high moral order and so the rightful guardians of the nursery. The infant she carried, he assured her, was a primal, a primitive (much as Her Great Majesty's peripheral subjects), little more than a savage in need of domestication, a colt to be broken in, a young animal to be tamed. He who'd rid a great empire of infant dysentery, how could he be doubted? Rose's hand went nervously to her belly where the infant kicked furiously in response. She flicked forward quickly to the 1950s: ah, infant re-imaged, now as fragile flower to be loved, delicate plant to be nurtured. Her hand sought her belly again where her infant had stilled and basked calmly, and so she seized the peace that offered, closed her eyes too and dozed.

Late. The days snailed by, every hour a year, and every twinge a hoped-for contraction. Her belly so enormous that she couldn't see her feet when she stood, not even when she sat and stretched her swollen legs out before her. A man had walked on the moon, while she had to pause four times as she climbed the stairs. The infant paid no heed to time, slept through noon, then, in the dead of night, woke her from restless sleep to kick and cavort inside her. Sometimes she leaned her belly against Pete's back — what a mere bit part he'd played in all of this — kicked him too, yes, if only in futile revenge. But while her husband tossed slightly and muttered, he slept soundly on. She hadn't anticipated this delay, rather had feared an unscheduled delivery.

'What if I start early? It happens occasionally. A woman delivered last week on her kitchen floor, another a month ago by a taxi man on the N7 verge. Could you cope?'

He'd looked aghast, but they'd never feared this, no, not this, this endless, endless wait. She pottered slowly round the house, indulged in comfort food, made cup after cup of tea, ate chocolate bars and cream-filled biscuits, and, to help pass the time, flicked through the papers and magazines Pete brought her. Yet she couldn't for some reason get interested in, be party to, the public frenzy that the Eurovision had transmitted from Dublin, and *in colour*, or grow eager for magazine advice on next summer tans and bikini fashions, for she somehow occupied an altogether different and excluded space. At times she sat in the nursery, read the baby care book yet again, until its litany of what might go wrong wearied; on other occasions she went to the bedroom where she kept her suitcase and checked once more that she'd stored everything inside.

Most of the time she sat for long hours alone, her left hand on her giant belly as she talked softly to the unknown that lived inside her, talked gently and asked what it feared and why it delayed to birth, while far, far away *Ryan's Daughter* had won two Oscars, Tom Kilroy's *The Big Chapel* had been shortlisted for the Booker Prize, and the generous Willy Brandt had been mentioned for a Nobel. Yes, up North – she sighed wearily at the thought – civilians had been massacred yet again – McConville ... Ballymurphy, they'd even introduced internment without trial – but the North and the border were far away too, and they mustn't fear, for all was safe and secure down South, down here. The phone rang shrilly in a manner that made her jump.

'Pete?'

'How goes it?'

'It doesn't.' She was so fed up. 'I know,' she shouted.

'Yes. Still here. I know. No, nothing. I told you I'd call if I'd started. No, nothing. No, nothing yet.'

It was Wednesday and dark when she finally woke to the waters that streamed down her thighs then settled in a warm pool beneath her. She felt the infant kick high up inside her in a manner that made the flimsy cotton jump as she pulled it over her head. She placed her two feet firmly on the ground, then steadied herself to balance her giant swollen womb, then slowly stood upright. Dark outside, save for a full moon that hung low in a starless sky. She dressed, then went to the spare room to check the hospital suitcase yet again: underwear, nightdresses, dressing gown, body creams, all there, with nappies too; how tiny the white cotton vests were, how minute the white towelled babygros.

'Hi.' Pete stood in the doorframe. 'Can't sleep again? Make you a cuppa?'

'I've started.'

'Great.' He stood awkward, unsure what to do next. She sensed he wanted to hug her, but the huge bulk that swelled between them made that impossible. Instead he just took her hand and squeezed it, and his damp palm told her he was as nervous as she was. 'Yeah, time to go in, but look, I'm fine, no pain, and no contractions yet.'

He drove her through the night city, its streets damp with recent rain. She felt strangely calm, hands folded on her belly. How little she knew of the mystery that lay ahead, of the unknown she now faced, of the infant soon to be born, of its wellbeing, its vulnerabilities, its talents, its strengths.

Contractions. Ten minutes apart, then seven, then five.

She paced the long hospital corridors, up and down, down and up, close to the chrome wall bar which she occasionally clutched, fearful of slipping on the shiny lino floor. Other women, in labour too, passed by, a girl, barely seventeen, a white-haired woman, both half-smiled silently her way as if in ancient female conspiracy, then passed on. At other times she sat in the ward chair, its straight back uncomfortable, and, as the midwife returned, lay on the bed yet again, heard the loud rattle the curtain rings made then felt the cold jelly that caused her to draw breath as they leaned heavy on her in search of the foetal heart.

'Go and have lunch, Pete, it'll be some time yet.'

'Prefer to stay here.'

'Go. Oh Christ, again.' Pain came in waves, and she clung desperately to the bar behind the bed and moaned. Door opened as nurses left and she suddenly heard everyday sounds again, the rattle of lunch cutlery, a disembodied radio voice that read the midday news, another bomb up North, a famine, this time in Biafra, then two jingo ads for cornflakes and cheese. All-enveloping pain again, oh not so soon again. She strained to see her watch, every two minutes now, then heard Pete shout for a nurse. Being wheeled then, along corridors and in lifts, a stranger's voice from somewhere that called 'good luck', then gas, masked medics and pain again.

'Don't push. You're not fully dilated yet.'

'I have to.'

Every fibre of her being wanted to do so. She pulled the useless gas away, as the pain owned her. 'I have to,' she screamed, 'don't you tell me what to do.' How she hated them all then, the monster child in the bloated body whose birth demanded this, the alien fingers that probed high up inside her, Pete who hovered helplessly nearby, the sickly sweet midwife who shoved the gas mask over her mouth again. 'Don't push. Not yet. It won't be long more, I promise.'

'Head fully engaged. Push now. Push. Push.'

Relief at last to do as they bid.

'Pant now, faster, faster, pant, pant. Head through, right shoulder, full torso, long body here, hey, someone'll be tall. Yes. Congratulations. You have a daughter.'

'Ann,' she smiled, 'welcome to our world.'

They placed her newborn on her belly. From where Rose lay she could see the fine ribs of black blood-streaked hair that clung to her scalp, while her arms and legs jerked and flayed; then she heard her cry with a loud wail. The nurse held the umbilical cord and nodded towards Pete, and Rose saw him take the small scissors, his hands clammy with fear, then cut his daughter free. Rose stretched out her hand, and placed a finger in that tiny palm, felt the newborn hand curl slowly around it, noted those fingers that were long and perfectly formed, marvelled at the small pink nails, their half-moon circles white at each cuticle. Then they took the newborn from her, and Rose feared the sucking sounds followed by soft whimpers that came from her right, until her newborn, now mucus-free, cried again and she lay back pleased that the child still yearned for the comfort she promised. She smiled up at Pete.

'Our love made flesh.'

'You're my heroine, Rose.'

'Full term plus six. Eight pounds, two ounces.'

Placenta came away, it slid painlessly between her thighs liver-coloured and enormous, its umbilical cord coiled thick and grey.

Infant returned to her mother, eyes closed, a small heartbeat that thumped steadily.

How peaceful she now looked after such an epic travail, then she turned her head and made sucking gestures with her lips. Rose lifted her to her right breast and secured mouth to nipple, felt her suck vigorously as a thin stream of blue-white milk flowed between her lips while some dribbled down her chin. New mother. New daughter. And it was good.

Everything changed. The new life that Rose held crooked in her arm stretched out before her, for henceforth, into a distant future, no day would pass that she wouldn't give thought to her daughter's welfare. Was the baby feeding, were her nappies right, what did that new cry mean, was she hungry, damp, or even in pain? Milestones too, the day she first stood, first walked, and cut her first tooth, birthdays with cakes and candles, balloons and presents, Christmas with the Infant Jesus and Santa Claus. A first day at school, then the kind tooth fairy. Reading and writing and school reports. Holidays with spades and sandcastles by the sea. Rose ran her finger down the soft pink cheek, so small, so vulnerable, so wanted, and so loved. Two large grey eyes lifted long, curled lashes and looked straight up at her, then the newborn head lolled again as she went back to sleep. The new mother lifted her carefully, heard her whimper briefly as she settled her into the Moses basket and covered her softly with a blanket. She sat on the side of the bed for a time and watched her. And a sudden wish to make her life safe and secure flooded through her. A year previously Ann hadn't existed, hadn't even been imagined. And now. Everything was changed. Rose was a mother.

8

Rose listened as the copper pennies dropped loudly into the gas metre, listened for Ann's cry, ever listened, knew that even as she dozed or snatched an hour or two of sleep that she still listened. Match wouldn't strike, box damp, she tried again, ah, at last, then lit the gas wick and saw it blaze blue-yellow with some satisfaction. What comfort a bath promised to her aching body, nipples that hung sore over belly flab and to the stitched cut between her thighs that still ached dully. She paused momentarily in quiet pleasure to view the return of her toes, except for the nails, how they'd grown, she must snatch a few seconds to cut them, and soon.

How welcome the warmth that enveloped her from the rising steam that also drizzled in narrow rivulets down the colder window pane and misted up the damp mirror beside it. She climbed gingerly into the hot bath, felt alright to her toes as she lowered herself slowly down, ouch, too hot for her bum, turned on the cold tap, waited, then lowered herself again. Comforting. Almost as good as that distant utopian dream of an unbroken night's sleep. She listened again as she soaped her hands, no infant's cry, at least not yet, then lay back in the luxurious warmth and closed her eyes.

When Rose woke it was dark outside, the bathwater cold. What time was it? How long had she slept? She didn't know. Her watch on the window sill read seven beneath its damp face, ten past to be precise. Was it day or night? And Ann? She listened for her cry, no sound, as she rushed to the Moses basket where her daughter stirred in restless sleep, whimpered briefly then slept on. And the empty double bed and darkened lounge confirmed that Pete wasn't home. Another quick calculation: if it were dawn, Pete would be here. So it was dusk. Eventide. Ten after seven, that was all. Or was it? She shivered, for, over a short period, she had lost all sense of time.

Farther down the coast, by Greystones and Arklow, fishermen worked and rested, their time defined by moon cycles and the ebb and flow of the sea's tide. Inland, in the Wicklow valleys and hills, farmers sowed to the day–night cycle of light and dark, when later they would reap, as their scythe cut through fields of autumn wheat. Dotted between them, the monastic spire of Glendalough pealed to God's time as it summoned to medieval prayer, to celebrate a rare saint's feast day, or yet another sinner's burial. While in Dublin, in the city, where the time was man-made, no darkness reigned, as neon signs blazed their colourful inducements all night through.

Rose now occupied a time outside all of these. One that was beyond those times and went back to a most ancient epoch, a time as yet invisible and shrouded in silence, one that had existed before the fisher folk and their moon tide ways, prior to the farmers and their daily night–day cycles, distant too from the churchgoers' cycle of Advent, Lent and Pentecost, long, long before the cities and their twenty-four-hour all-light global clock, for it had existed with and survived all of these. For the time she now inhabited was goddess time, being female breast and body defined, gifted with the intuitive knowing that breast milk spelt food, that food spelt survival, and most of all, that these two spelt life's eternal renewal.

Each time Rose woke since her daughter's birth, at times to a dark and silent room, she woke to breasts that were hard and engorged with milk. Woke and listened for the cry that she knew would come, for her newborn call that always did. Listened for and heard her whimper, then cry more loudly, a hungry cry that by now she had learnt to distinguish from her discomfort cry, and from her pain cry, and on so hearing, she, no matter how tired, went wearily to lift the crying child and fixed her to her left nipple. The child always grasped it, then moved her head in frustration as it slipped from between her tiny lips, while her mother pressed the nipple firmly into her opened mouth again, and the infant, so hungry, began to suck. An excess of milk usually spewed out first, some into her mouth, and her small throat muscle throbbed as she swallowed, while a little dribbled down her chin and dampened her babygro. Then she would suck again and swallow it all, and continue to suck rhythmically.

Rose liked to close her eyes as the milk flowed from her, and savour the sensual and pleasurable sensations that it brought. She then held the child closer as she walked to the press and extracted a nappy, clean vest and babygro, and stroked Ann's head softly as she continued to feed, contented. Then to wash and change her, then they both might sleep again, for a whole three or more hours.

Yet, before long, a too-silent child made Rose fearful again, so she'd tiptoe into the room and check that she still breathed, and she'd stand and watch her tiny chest rise and fall and know with some relief that she lived. On other occasions her newborn cried for no reason she could establish, an event that left her frantic with worry. Colic, the downstairs tenant had suggested in a throwaway voice as if that were merely trivial, claimed that many children suffered from it, suggested Rose let her cry away, not be fearful, and know that she'd be fine. But Rose couldn't bring herself to do that when the fed, winded, changed and comforted infant still cried on. Was she ill, sickening for something terrible? Rub her back for wind yet again, hear the burp as another mouthful of regurgitated milk spilt down her shoulder, pace the floor for a time, sit down and soothe her, try putting her in the basket and rock her there, and wish, just wish she might tell her new mother what exactly was wrong.

Rose knew she had to buy something to wear to the christening, for her post-baby body looked swamped in the flowing materials of her pregnancy tents, yet she was still too large to fit into anything she'd worn before that time. Her body shape had changed too, her breasts now enormous while her belly remained flabby. And the shaved stubble of her pubic hair still bore traces of the purple antiseptic they'd painted on her vulva for the delivery (it had merely faded to a dull puce on several scrubbings), while her re-grown pubic stubble was hard and wiry, it itched atrociously and left her desperate to scratch there, and risk being arrested should she do so in public.

And she knew, no matter how often she showered, that she smelt, of milk and baby puke and yukky nappies, while Grace, who behaved as if infants arrived from heaven by stork, had no understanding whatever, an illusion that her newborn strengthened by cooing angelically each time her friend called. Not that Pete was any better, with his endless assurances of 'I know, I know' (when he didn't know at all) and the helpless hangdog look he assumed as he dared voice an opinion. Yet come Saturday, at his instigation, even his insistence, she reluctantly left the infant and a supplementary bottle with her husband and went into town with Grace to buy a dress for her daughter's christening day.

'This one.' Grace, being Grace, insisted they start at Brown T's. She shoved Rose into a changing room then proceeded to supply her with the dresses she'd selected. 'Yes, this.'

'Too fussy. I'd prefer something simple that'll hide my bumps. And definitely not that, I want to tone down my bust, not draw attention to it.'

'I think that's nice. Well, maybe in another colour.'

'It's too tight, try for a larger size.'

'Sixteen! You can't possibly be sixteen, Rose, at your height.'

'You just don't understand being a mother.'

'No, but I have a sense of occasion. No, wrong size again and all wrong around the bust. Try this and make virtue of your new-found tits.'

'I'm just terrified my milk will leak and that I'll have to buy something that costs the earth.'

'Yes, definitely, this one is you.'

'Far too expensive. Won't wear it much again, don't expect to be this shape forever.'

'Oh damn the cost, it's a once-off occasion, you've got to look your loveliest. Can't have my godchild magnificent in crochet and lace with her mother there wondering whether her own dress will wash.'

'Look, I'm taking this, it'll do me fine.'

'Not bad. Hmm, maybe. Like the floral print, the colour suits you too, and it's a nice sunny yellow, the drawstring under your bust might be tightened or loosened.'

It was the best she'd tried on, one she felt comfortable inside, but she couldn't summon up much enthusiasm from the fearful concerns that flooded her mind. Could Pete cope? Would he wait for the formula to heat? Would her daughter suck from a rubber teat? Would it give too slow a flow of milk, or maybe too fast? What if she rejected the formula, what if it made her ill? Or maybe she'd like it too much and reject the breast when she returned. 'I need to get home,' she pleaded.

'No way, I've got further plans.'

'I need to get home, Grace. This is my first time away from her.'

'Look, I'm under orders, Pete's insisted. Anyway, we've got to get shoes, can't buy them without you trying them on.'

'Then I need to phone him, just to check. Please.'

She did, dropped four pennies into the public phone, heard them clang loudly then pulled the booth's door shut on the street noise outside and on Grace. 'Everything alright?' she shouted down the receiver.

'Fine. Finished the bottle then went back to sleep.'

'You changed her, and if the babygro was damp you changed that too? Don't put her down with her bib still on, that's dangerous, it might cover her face.'

'Relax. All done. You've married a new man.'

'So what are you doing now?'

'Reading the paper, business section. Enjoy yourself, everything here's just fine.'

'Shoes next.' Grace dragged her into Fitzpatrick's.

'You'll bring your new lover boy to the christening?'

she asked as she tried on a first pair.

Grace smiled coyly but shook her head. 'Not ready for that yet.'

Rose sighed as she reached for a second pair. So they were still at the gruesome twosome phase, just wanted to be alone together, eyeball to eyeball en route to their great operatic crescendo of utopian sex. Well, she and Pete had their love made flesh now, yet she sighed wistfully as she walked up and down by the floor mirror to view her still-swollen feet as they hung out over the shoes' sophisticated sides. 'Just had a baby,' she murmured apologetically to no one in particular, then shook her head at the mirror.

'How about these, then?' Grace dangled a pair of toeless cream sandals, impossibly high-heeled, their instep decorated with a small yellow flower that matched her new dress perfectly.

'I need something comfortable.'

'You can't cave in on appearances after just one kid, you're only allowed do that nowadays after you've had at least six.'

'Cream, flat and comfortable, but dressy,' the assistant smiled cheerfully. 'Now I know what you want. Certainly, ma'am. And on sale offer if possible.'

Tissue paper crinkled as Grace extracted the edge of the new dress and held it against them. 'Hmm, might just get away with it.'

'They'll do fine,' she agreed hurriedly, before Grace could change her mind. 'Many thanks.'

Rose stood by the ancient baptismal font at the rear of the church, distant from the high altar where she and Pete had first exchanged their vows, saw its wide bowl gape cold, atop a base embossed with winged cherubs that frolicked between marble leaves. She waited as padre lit the *Pax Christi* candle that stood beside it and watched the dull grey smoke curl from its blood-red message and heavenwards. Did Christ know how tired she was, so tired, more tired than even a male saviour might comprehend? And no pew nearby, not even a chair to sit on. She glanced towards Ann nervously, her small head resting on Pete's shoulder, fearful that she would cry, then saw the padre beckon Grace and Joe as godparents towards him. Why had Grace chosen to wear a small hat, a ridiculous blue thing with a net forehead veil, while Joe, who she'd seldom seen since he'd been their best man, just looked awkward beside her in a casual jacket and slacks.

'This infant,' the padre explained in a hushed whisper as he nodded towards her daughter, 'has been born of nature and sin. Christian baptism will cleanse her of that, and she will then be born again, of Christ and the Holy Spirit.'

Grace nodded eagerly in agreement as her small hat bobbed on her head, and Rose saw Pete hand the infant to her, and watched as the sign of the cross was made on her forehead.

'Do you, as godparents, renounce the devil on her behalf, and all his works and pomps?'

'We do,' the godparents intoned.

The priest's lace cuff brushed against the sleeping child, her eyes flickered, she whimpered briefly, then her eyes closed again and she slept on. Rose watched Grace hold the infant out over the font, saw the long christening robe flow down her arm, watched her manicured red nails pull back the christening shawl, as the cold water trickled onto Ann's forehead and clung in tiny droplets to her hair's dark strands.

'I baptise you,' the padre intoned, 'in the name of the father and of the son and of the Holy Spirit, amen.'

The born-again Ann opened her eyes wide and cried loudly. Oh why, Rose wondered, hadn't he heated the water, and what would she do now, when that was clearly a hungry cry and she once more needed to be fed. The priest smiled nervously her way, shook her husband's hand then paused to chat once more with the new godparents.

'That's it?' Rose asked nervously.

'Yes, the ritual is complete.'

'I'll take her,' Rose said quickly, 'wait here for me, be back shortly.' Why had she decided so vehemently that her child would never have a soother? Should have bought one, well, just for this occasion. She sat into a distant pew and jigged her daughter up and down in a futile effort to silence her. To her left a bent woman prayed in loud whispers to Saint Jude, while a teenage couple placed one red rose on the nearby shrine of Saint Valentine. Despite Ann's continued loud wails, neither glanced her way. Beyond them, Saint Teresa, the mystic of Lisieux from close by Flanders fields, proffered yellow and white roses of friendship and peace. A nearby confessional door banged loudly; a penitent, shriven too of his sins, emerged from behind green baize to kneel in prayer, his gnarled hand fingering a rosary. A schoolgirl approached the Madonna's shrine, genuflected, placed a lit candle before it, then walked back slowly to rejoin a friend. The statue towered high above all, the same Virgin Mother as she had visited at Monserrat, feet firmly grounded on a serpent-free earth, a triumphant mother, crowned, and with sceptre outstretched. She'd understand, wouldn't she? Rose slowly loosened the drawstring on her dress and lifted the full breast from it, then placed the upright nipple between her infant's lips, felt the child's relieved suck. The two schoolgirls blushed and giggled, then they and the penitent left. Only the two lovers remained. Ten minutes later, Rose and her sleeping child left too.

They returned to the flat, where Grace laid out food she had brought for the celebration, dainty nibbles of small crackers topped with white prawns, pink salmon and black caviar, all sprinkled with a minute scattering of chopped green parsley. Rose registered her friend's relief that the crackers had remained crisp and that her thimbleful pourings of expensive white wine were adequately chilled. She had also brought a cake, which she had iced white with baby storks and tiny pink winged angels atop, and, as Rose cut the first slice and gave it to Pete it fell away to almond icing, then heavy fruit, cherries and nuts. Joe, not to be outdone, produced champagne and poured the fizzy liquid into the silver christening mug, and, as it cascaded down the side, they circled the Moses basket, then passed the mug one to another to sip and share.

'A toast too,' Grace called, and Joe poured again, this time into glasses that they clinked together and raised high over the sleeping infant.

'To Ann'

'To Ann.'

'I'm the fairy godmother at your crib,' cried Grace, 'may you have long life, health and good fortune.'

Rose lay in the bed and watched Pete as he rubbed his daughter's back, then stroke her head and face and whisper 'go to sleep, my precious, go to sleep,' then wrap her tightly in her blanket, set her down in her basket and rock it to and fro. Ann's large blue eyes followed the butterflies that swayed above her, then closed as she went to sleep. Rose continued to watch him as he busied himself around the room, lifted clothes from the floor and placed them in the wash basket, tidied the baby wipes and cotton buds away then closed the window and drew the curtains over. She watched him undress, a shadowy form from an almost forgotten past, saw him pull off his tie and cast it from him, then open his shirt to reveal the hairs matted there. He removed his trousers swiftly, then paused briefly to remove his watch, where the band of skin beneath it flashed white against his freckled arm. The bed creaked quietly as he climbed in and she moved closer to him.

'Hi.'

'Hi.'

'Well done, great day.'

'Thanks. You too.'

'I want you,' she said suddenly. 'I've missed you so.'

'Remember how we once were?'

'Try me,' she smiled.

Afterwards she slept 'til dawn when Pete's discarded watch told her that their daughter had slept through the night.

'Went out for a short run and brought you back this.' He placed a spring of blood thorn on the table close by her. 'Help you remember back to that very first kiss.'

'And you put some in my wedding bouquet too.'

'And now, cook you breakfast. Full Irish?'

She savoured the smell that wafted towards her, of sizzling bacon, browned sausages, and button mushrooms.

'Here's to a full night's sleep again.' She held out her mug for tea and her husband grinned and then nodded.

9

Rose knew Brendan long before he entered Grace's radar, although as Mr Foley.

'*I* don't know *you*, do I?' He'd looked at her keenly with cold blue eyes as if to ascertain which part of her anatomy was dysfunctional.

Rose Leahy. Pharmacist. Returned from maternity leave.'

'Oh. That.'

She recalled what she'd heard of him at work as his tall theatre-gowned frame ambled away, knew that he'd already climbed several greasy career ladders as if such were a life calling. Forever surprised, she surmised, once he reached the top of one ladder to find that it merely led to the bottom rung of the next. From the top of his class leaving school to college fresher among five hundred others, invisible, unnoticed and unknown. From *summa cum laude* graduation to harassed junior doc. And now, with his new consultancy post, on a bottom rung again, consultant surgeon, specialising in, well, to start, being on Camilla's ward, in gallbladders. Yet, at long last, peacock style, with the final summit of a full consultancy post, his born-to-be-mine natural habitat within sight. Always at his worst when on that loathed bottom rung again. No one that mattered even remotely below him (a mere amorphous mass to be trampled on and controlled), and with all those steep steps yet to climb. And was also famed for changing his woman at every ladder shift. So, as per script, enter a new partner, and oh no, who else but Grace. Rose suffered a stab of guilt at the level of mean satisfaction she felt inside; Grace was a poor choice for the hospital's latest control freak.

Over the week that followed, as Rose harboured her secret knowledge she listened to hospital gossip in which he frequently featured with greater interest than usual.

'And how are we today, Mrs Brown?' Foley was known to feign a geniality older than his years, but only with patients. 'Let's see it, neat scar now, isn't it, your diet sheet, and yes, you may bring your salvaged gallstones home, have them for you in this small jar here.' For he was irate with staff, hated Sullivan, the hospital manager, fought with matron, and worst of all, clashed with the elderly and much respected senior consultant Wyndham.

Rose watched as Foley closed the window firmly shut then glanced around the room, past the portrait of the red-garbed Lord Aynesbury, the august hospital benefactor, beyond the small altar to the Virgin Mary, to pause briefly at where matron sat, then quickly move on, until Rose felt his clinical gaze pause and rest on her. 'I know you from somewhere other than here, don't I?' it asked with a slight puzzled look.

She coloured, glanced down at her file and feigned to read, as he moved to Sullivan. They had in fact met socially three times, at a dinner party in Grace's apartment, at a hospital charity binge, and at a cocktail do only the week before that Grace had insisted she and Pete attend.

'Shall we begin?' Rose saw Sullivan turn to matron, a gesture accepted with a nod by Wyndham, as one of old-world courtesy to a lady. 'What complaints have you for us this month?' he asked as Foley tapped the table impatiently.

'Three in all, one from the ward staff and three from patients.'

'I'll take the staff first,' he agreed with a smile.

'The matter as to who is to water the patients' flowers and plants has arisen again,' explained matron. 'Able-bodied patients choose to do it themselves, and despite several prominent notices on hygiene, many still leave an unhygienic mess of mud, stalks and insects in the bathrooms. And I do not need to emphasise the importance of hygiene here. It cannot wait for the cleaners, the nurse aides say it is outside their contract, and my nursing staff simply don't have time. Might we,' she asked hopefully, 'employ one person with sole responsibility for this task hospital-wide?'

'Ban flowers and plants on ward,' interjected Foley forcefully. He waved his arm grandly. 'Let them eat chocolate.'

'For a start, I find it preferable we exclude the unions from this.' Wyndham glanced around the table for support. Rose lowered her gaze as the others nodded. 'A new recruit? Who pays? Whose budget is it drawn from? Not mine, I assure you. However, I do accept, matron, that the hygiene issue must be fully addressed.'

'It would help if I had the weight of this meeting behind me when I raise it with the staff nurses again,' said matron hopefully.

'Of course, I've noted your points,' said Sullivan calmly. 'And the issues raised by patients, matron?'

'Two. They both relate to the religious ethos of the hospital.'

'Perhaps you'd give us your views on these,' Wyndham addressed Rose, 'you being young and of the Catholic persuasion.'

'I've had representations from a Methodist patient,' matron

continued quickly. 'She objects to the rosary being delivered by tannoy into her ward each evening. She emphasises her respect for Catholic beliefs, merely does not want its cult of Mary imposed on her. And certainly not four hours after her hysterectomy. She's very irate. I'm fearful that if she doesn't get a satisfactory apology she may phone Gay Byrne. The second complaint related to the church oratory and suggests that we desist from displaying a large purple Lenten cloth with "repent" sewn on it in resplendent gold close by the maternity ward.'

'They know we are a Catholic hospital,' said Sullivan wearily, 'and whereas we are happy to accept non-Catholics as patients, they must accept that our Catholic ethos prevails.'

'Your views, Ms Leahy?' Wyndham nodded towards Rose, who glanced frantically towards matron.

'Can I assure them,' she intervened quickly, 'that I've brought the matter to the meeting's attention and that it's being addressed?'

'Of course,' he nodded courteously. 'And Ms Leahy?'

'Might we get on with it,' asked Foley testily. 'What was the other complaint about?'

'The TVs on ward.'

'Take them off all wards,' demanded Foley irritably. 'Eight cantankerous patients, three who want to sleep, two to read, and they can't do either as long as the rest squabble and can't agree as to the station to watch.'

'This patient,' matron raised a letter, 'dislikes the popular *Riordans* programme. He didn't find Batty Brennan's instructions as to how to lay horse manure as fertiliser conducive to his healing.'

'I've noted your points.' Sullivan nodded solemnly as he

scribbled in the jotter before him.

'I've every confidence in your ability to address these matters, matron,' said Wyndham kindly.

Sullivan turned to Rose next and she felt relief. The meeting she had to attend quarterly, and so soon after her maternity break, found her struggling to re-adjust to hospital life. 'We move on?' he asked. 'Ms Leahy, please.'

'Could the doctors, when they plan to change pharmaceutical brands, tell me in advance, so I can arrange to have the new brands in stock?'

'The Health Department prefers,' Wyndham interjected, 'out of deference to the taxpayer, that when brands are identical in substance, the cheaper are prescribed. It's preferable,' he glanced towards Foley, 'that our medical staff respect that.'

'It's not for me,' said Rose firmly, 'to decide what is prescribed. But I need to know in advance to assure that what is prescribed is in stock.'

It happened at times with new intakes, the young and ambitious doctors, who wished to display their up-to-date research knowledge, left her trying to contact them urgently when they'd failed to inform her accurately of their preferences.

'Are an inordinate number of contraceptives still being prescribed?' asked Wyndham testily. 'I cannot believe that so many south Dublin women have suddenly developed irregular menstrual cycles.'

'I administer as prescribed,' said Rose firmly.

'This is hardly a matter for Ms Leahy,' said Foley hotly. 'And I reserve the right to prescribe as I please. Damn the Vatican.'

'My concerns,' Wyndham's expression told Rose he was

angry, 'are medical, I assure you, not religious. And I am concerned, and my concerns are ongoing, about the over-prescription of new medicines for young mothers when we do not yet have adequate research results as to their long-term effects Also, we are heavily state-funded and are most certainly obliged to obey the law of the land.' Rose sensed he disliked Foley intensely, for, over and above the unthinking arrogance of the younger consultant, his inference that Wyndham's concerns were other than medical had incensed the older man.

Any further issues from or for pharmacy, Ms Leahy?' asked Sullivan smoothly.

She shook her head, silence prevailed and Rose sighed softly with relief.

'There is a matter I wish to explore further.' Wyndham spoke carefully. 'Might we have an explanation about the patient' ... he lifted a file and handed it to Sullivan ... 'nine-year-old youth. You recall the case?'

Sullivan nodded as he flicked through the pages.

'Feed of green apples,' Wyndham continued, 'raided an orchard, I believe. It seems we inadvertently removed his appendix. A child submitted to a general anaesthetic, and a perfectly good appendix was removed, by a full emergency team who were summoned in at 4 a.m. By you, Mr Foley, I believe. Might we have your version of this and some explanation as to your over-eagerness to yield the knife?'

'When?' asked Foley coldly. 'I don't honestly recall any such event.'

'You're called in at 4 a.m. frequently?' pressed Wyndham.

'Of course not. I need to check the relevant file.'

Sullivan pushed a file towards him and the room fell

silent save for the soft swish of pages as he read. Wyndham glanced around the table. No one spoke. No one planned to, either. Rose dared glance towards Foley, who sat, back erect, and refused to look chastened.

'Might I have an explanation?' pressed Wyndham.

'I do not see it as a matter for this meeting,' said Foley eventually.

'Of course, I can take it further if you wish.'

Silence fell again.

'Perhaps we might adjourn this meeting,' matron glanced hopefully towards Sullivan, 'and permit Mr Wyndham and Mr Foley to continue their discussion privately.'

Sullivan glanced towards the senior Wyndham, who shook his head curtly as silence fell again.

'I was on night duty and present as the youth was admitted,' Rose interjected eventually. 'I'd been called up to A&E, where they needed penicillin urgently. I heard the agency nurse ask the youth if he knew what might have caused his pain. I heard him say no. His father was with him, said he didn't know either. I distinctly heard both father and son say that.'

'He had all the symptoms of appendicitis,' Foley added quickly, 'other than high fever. What else was I to do? It was only on ward afterwards that he boasted triumphantly of his orchard raid.'

Outside a lawnmower rumbled distantly, and beyond that Rose heard the low hum of passing traffic. Foley's hand still held the file, knuckles white. 'Your explanation is accepted,' Wyndham said at last.

'Meeting adjourned,' said Sullivan hurriedly.

Grace, Rose thought as she gathered up her files, *that was for you. As for you, lover boy*, she glanced towards Foley, *you owe me.*

As a medic, Grace's new love knew all that could go wrong with women's bodies, a topic he had studied over many years, and been well awarded for his knowledge of same. Indeed, he had won the Benjamin Woodridge memorial prize for his paper on *Advances in Surgical Procedures: The Gallbladder and Neighbouring Organs*. He'd also won the Reynolds-Wynne gold medal as first in his junior consultancy year. And, as surgeon, he took ongoing delight at the prospect of slicing off cancerous breasts, while he most envied his gynaecological colleagues who whipped out fibrous wombs, and unblocked infertile fallopians, while he champed endlessly at the bit to progress upwards beyond mere gallbladders.

Yet, since he was seventeen, Brendan had always retained one woman in his life outside the realms of those over whom he might, however brilliantly, yield the knife. Megan, who'd begun college with grades every bit as dazzling as his, had partnered him through his undergrad years, but come final year had dropped back in the testosterone-driven race and chosen, to his amazement, to settle for general practice.

'How could you, Megan? Settle for being a lowly GP? Waste your professional life on that dull trail of neurotic suburbans who do little more exciting than occasionally run a mild temperature, cough quietly, and sneeze.'

Shortly after graduation, he met Linda, every bit as ambitious as him, until the hours expected of budding gynaecologists just wore her out.

Whereas Megan had been dazzled by his success in a field similar to her own and Linda had been blinded by his array of awards and medals, he was perturbed to find that Grace was wholly unenthralled by such trophies. No,

Grace, who warbled 'all you need is love' as she dragged him to bed (and even seemed to believe it), was so different from her predecessors.

Grace, now so successful herself in business, where success was measured by profits, by accumulated capital, and by large financial bonuses while Brendan merely earned a salary and fees, if reasonably good ones. But she was in love, and she never once questioned the laws of the heart that dictated how little status and money had to do with all that. Juan, after all, had the earning power of a beach bum when she'd first lost her virginity to him, and her secret and intense liaison with Father Y had been with a lowly cleric who had been solemnly bound by a poverty vow.

What Grace's lack of enthrallment did was to leave her in some way outside her lover's control, a new experience with which Brendan struggled to grapple. Within a few short weeks she had grown from an interesting diversion to a potential liaison, to being an obsession, a state that left him with a terrifying fear of being trapped. For Grace seemed, if unwittingly, to press fantasy buttons on Brendan's elegant suit that plunged him into a dependent state and belief that he somehow wouldn't survive, *on his terms*, without her, while the growing intensities of the lust that she evoked in him and the pleasures it brought found him incapable of letting her go.

While work presented a ready escape from her inner presence, not so the balm of sleep as she also began to haunt his dreams. Grace, when she didn't occupy his bed, began to appear nightly to his sleeping self in a variety of guises, sometimes as a giant octopus whose myriad flaying legs enveloped and trapped him. On other occasions she stretched beneath him as a marshy bog, into which he sank deep, inescapably deeper, or at other times as a naked goddess with her back turned to him, and a glance that hinted at coy flirtatiousness, and from which he knew he should flee while his body, terrifyingly, refused to follow the dictates of his fine scientific and rational mind and do so. On waking, when that same mind kicked into action, he simply couldn't comprehend his plight. And as it appraised Grace's assets with the cold eye of science, he concluded that she was attractive, yes, but hardly one of those great beauties by whom men, even those greater than he, had historically become hopelessly mesmerised, far from it. For she was in no way perfect, a woman now in her early thirties with non-American teeth that were European crooked, with a neck that hinted at wrinkles, a belly slightly given to fat, and ankles about to thicken. He tried, for the first of many times, to end it. She didn't weep, just smiled quietly and said, 'you'll be back.'

He was. How had she known that? Her knowledge, so superior to his in this regard, undermined him further.

Finally he sought out a male colleague with whom he might discuss his problem, a task that took some time, as the chat of their social encounters seldom veered beyond medical promotions and sport. When he finally tracked down an old friend for whom he bought a quiet gin as he confided, he was duly diagnosed as 'addicted'; for which insight the friend bought his colleague a gin back then proceeded to discuss the recently announced international rugby selections. But at least he had gained a medical term for his plight; he was, he now knew, secretly and shamefully just that: addicted. Belonged now with that ghastly sub-culture of binge eaters, boozers, snorters and liners, who yearned for endless intense highs and just couldn't break free. He would, though. He'd escape. He had to.

Meanwhile Grace, deluded enough to believe she knew her man, carried little sense of Brendan's true inner process. Indeed, his belief that she had trapped him would have left her taken aback, for Grace had no doubt that Brendan stayed with her of his own free will. He stopped over at her place, whenever he chose, and returned to his own pad any night he preferred to do that. She'd neither expected nor hinted that she expected expensive gifts that might cause him financial worry; in fact, attitudes to the jewellery cache Andy had bought her had made her wary of that, so much so that she positively wouldn't take any. She had no wish to marry, if he perceived that as a trap, and she most definitely did not want his child, which she accepted, if not mutually desired, might trap him too. She sought no verbal or written commitments from him, for his desire for her and hers for him was, she knew, enough.

Brendan's tendency to disappear for a bit now and then she shrugged off as due to pressures of work, an explanation with which he was more than happy to concur at each inevitable return, as he was drawn to the bed where he might satiate his raging lusts once more. Grace was also in no doubt that she satisfied him in a myriad of other ways too. With food, for few were her equal as cook, and having established his favourite dishes (lobster or duck, both served with a chilled white, followed by pear and almond tart laced with thick cream), she served them up with smiling delight. And with her selection of clothing, for she learnt early on that he favoured spicy Mediterranean colours, vibrant indigos, reds, yellows and oranges, that flattered her sallow skin tone. And most of all, with the coveted glances his friends made her way, the gaze that left her in no doubt that they envied him his good fortune, while knowing at the same time that she was his alone.

Her work situation had advanced too, for she had been selected to chair two significant committees within Import-Export, one that explored new initiatives within IT and the second that monitored potential expansions in the market, both with a particular emphasis on exports. This, with her ongoing managerial work, earned her a company car, a BMW (which she seldom drove for she still preferred to walk to work), share options, and the likelihood, at some future time, of a seat on the board. She toyed with the idea of selling her apartment and trading up – she definitely needed a bigger room to serve as a home study, and it seemed like a wise move to invest in a townhouse, but she drew back from such a venture. The comfort of her familiar apartment was all she knew as a secure home.

And there was music, more enchanting than ever now that she was in love again. She no longer just played her cassettes in the apartment and just listened; she sang, all those songs of love and its celebration, with Brendan ever present on her mind. 'If They Asked Me I Could Write a Book', 'Just in Time', 'There's a Small Hotel', 'Some Enchanted Evening', 'Bewitched, Dazzled and Bewildered', and so many more. The daily news might recount tales of ongoing horror from the North, a mere sixty miles up the road, women might act as honey traps there to lure soldier boys to their deaths, those who chose to love them instead might be tarred, feathered, and tied to lampposts; but, in the spring of '74 the North and its militants seemed far away, and despite its constant media headlines, she knew that she would never let her dream of great love go.

Ann, who's three, likes the crèche. She sits in a circle and holds hands, her hair tied in two bunches held with a blue band that matches her pale blue smock. She wears dark blue tights and sways to and fro as they all sing 'Ten Green Bottles' together. She has to let their hands go and hold up eight fingers when they get to 'eight', and she can't do it because both her thumbs always stick up too. She's better when they get to three and four, for she can count up to that, to four, the age she'll be at her next birthday, and hold up four fingers and sing at the same time. After, she takes green crayons and copies the number four on her page, then draws four bottles beside it, colours them in green, then writes her name, Ann, beside them. The pink and red crayons are gone, so she colours in her name in yellow, and the number four in brown, and is careful to stay inside the lines.

After, she cuts pictures of the moon and stars from a magazine, and glues them above the bottles, then sticks sparkly sequins in silver on them with more glue. She loves the silver sequins, even though they stick to her fingers with the glue, and spill a bit down her smock; and while it's night, she colours in a yellow sun and a blue sky beside them.

A small bell rings to say time to go outside, and she races to get to the scooter first, then scoots down the slope, faster than those on tricycles who try to race past her but can't. When it's someone else's turn, she goes to wait in line for her turn on the swing. Everyone gets five pushes, that's all, forward and back, forward and back, and the breeze tosses her hair and makes one of her bunches come loose. She digs in the sandpit for a bit too, fills a plastic dish shaped like a baby fish with sand and turns it over, then fills one shaped like a bigger fish and turns that over beside it.

Inside, her lunchbox contains a brown bread roll, yellow cheese, a small carton of fruit juice and an apple. She swaps her cheese furtively for five crisps and tries to stop the noise they make as she crunches them, then gets a quick drink of another's Coke in return for two bites from her apple. The bread roll tastes alright, mainly because she's still hungry.

At home she's daddy's girl, for he lifts her up to pin her drawing to the fridge door, then stands back and has a long and serious discussion with her as to how she made it. Come bedtime, he tells her a story; she likes the one when he pretends to be a monster beast like the big bad wolf who ate Red Riding Hood's granny, and the cross daddy bear who asked, 'And who's been eating my porridge?' and Snow White, who he pretends is named Snow Black with seven warts, even though she tells him over and over that her right name is Snow White. And then he always says that his favourite dwarf is 'Dozy', which she knows means it's time to go to sleep. Mam's just boring, as she tells her to wash her hands and scrub her teeth and blow her nose and eat her dinner, even the carrots which are yukky and she hates them. And calls up the stairs for the story to finish because it's time to say her prayers and Dad puts on the night light and tells her to close her eyes and say '... four angels at my head, Matthew, Mark, Luke and John, God bless the bed that I lie on.' When she's sick though, she wants Mam, and when the pain in her ear is bad and her

144

mam holds her to her soft self and rocks her to and fro and cries too as she gives her the medicine that makes it better.

At Grace's, her godmother shows her how to bake a gingerbread man. She climbs on the stool and hands down the sugar, flour and ginger, mixes them together, then cuts him out with the shape Grace gives her and watches him through the oven window as he cooks brown. When he's almost done, she selects colours from the smarties: blue for his eyes, pink for his nose, red for his mouth with orange buttons down his middle. She's careful too as she drops the melted chocolate to make them stick, also for his feet and hands, then she waits for him to cool. As they wait, Grace attempts to teach her to sing 'All Things Bright and Beautiful' but she prefers to play at the computer, type her name and watch it come out on a white sheet in small letters, then in bigger ones, and then in bigger letters still until she's filled the whole page. Grace plays a game with their new creation and sings 'Run, run, as fast as you can, you can't catch me, I'm your gingerbread man', and runs around the room and Ann chases her, and gets to eat him all up.

At weekends she goes with Dad and Mam to the park where they pause at the blood thorn tree. Sometimes, when she wears her wool coat and ear muffs and gloves the tree is bare, and she kicks her feet in the dry leaves beneath it and they dance up around her in the wind. Other times, when she wears her cardigan over her wool dress the sun shines through its red blossoms and dapples the ground there. When she wears her summer dress the red petals litter the ground and she dances on them in the sunlight. And when their berries come Mam gives her one to taste, and she bites into the cream-white food inside it and likes it.

Sometimes Dad races her from the tree to the railings and back, and she always gets back first and wins. That makes her laugh and laugh, for Mam claps and kisses her when she beats him and comes back first. Then they climb over the railway bridge to the beach where she races across the sand to the seashore and paddles in the cold waves that lap against her legs; then Dad buys her a ninety-nine with a flake and raspberry syrup to eat as they drive home again.

'Dark horse.' Rose heard laughter as she entered the canteen, followed by a buzz that revolved around a petite blonde intern nearby. 'And none of us guessed. Where's Brendan?'

'Brendan Foley?'

'Yeah, surprised everyone. Whirlwind. Together for just six weeks. Seen her solitaire? It's a dazzler. And, what's more, he's just been promoted again.'

'I believe congratulations are in order,' Rose observed coolly once she'd tracked him down to his office. The fact that they both knew he owed her gave her Dutch courage, and her voice remained calm for she was determined to contain the anger she felt. 'I was with Grace last week, she'd no inkling of this. You've told her?'

'Thanks for the good wishes.' His gaze returned to the record open before him. 'Stay out of it, Rose. Yes, I intend to write to your friend, Ms Donovan.'

'Write! You haven't even told her yet? You leave her to hear of your fiancée on some gossip grapevine? You might at least tell her to her face.'

'I can't.' He pushed the file away. 'I tried, believe me, and more than once.' A momentary terror flicked across his pale eyes. 'Ten minutes with her and all resolution fades. Look, Grace and I were never about marriage, we both knew that.'

'So, you'll keep her on as a …'

'No, it's over. Mary wouldn't have that and I don't intend to risk losing her. Now, if you'll forgive me,' he nodded towards the door, 'I've a busy day ahead and so doubtless have you.'

'No,' she retorted loudly, 'you'll hear me out.'

'No, *you'll* hear *me*. And,' he glanced towards the half-open door, 'keep your voice down. I've had more than enough drama in my life in recent times, I can do without you too.'

'Grace is my friend. I can't bear—'

'Look, you work here, you know how it is. Operate daily, on kids, when they're very ill, on young adults who may not live, on good mothers who may die too.' He smiled wanly. 'What if I even do a little good that way? And what I need, Rose, come evening, is rest, a quiet home, a gentle wife, and a nice meal with family.'

'Whoa! That's a sea change.'

'Grace is too much for me, I can't live at her pitch and progress my career as well. You work here, on the front line of who lives and who dies too, you must understand that. Grace's addiction to romantic drama, at the end of the day, how important is that? Now leave,' he nodded towards the door, 'I've said too much already. And by the way,' he gave another faint smile, 'thanks for the congratulations.'

Rose said nothing, for while she couldn't disagree with him, she was determined not to align with him and against her friend. 'But she'll feel so horribly betrayed,' she murmured at last.

'Look, she did matter, still does in fact. I've just made a difficult choice. Can't you see that? But I have made it. Since you're her friend, you'll keep an eye on her for me, won't you, at least until she adjusts. Yes, I'll have a cup,' he called as the tea lady appeared through the door, 'milk, no sugar, Mrs Ryan.'

'They're waiting, Mr Foley, matron and staff nurse waiting for you to do the rounds.'

'Thanks.' He threw back the tea and stood to leave.

Dear Grace, thought Rose as he bent his tall frame then walked out the door, *what are you to do?*

10

Rose lined up at the Abbey box office and waited impatiently to book tickets. How slowly the queue moved. She glanced at her watch again, five twenty, and she wanted to beat the weekend commuter move from the city. Still, Lorca's *Blood Wedding* had got rave reviews and she wanted to surprise Pete with a treat for their anniversary that was in some way different. She smiled quietly as she thought about her plan, how they'd come into the city and share a special meal at the Gresham, follow it with the theatre, then have a drink or two after when they'd discuss the play. Yet the bus strike made the weekend traffic even worse than usual, and on reflection she should have brought Ann with her, for the chances of picking her up at the crèche by six now seemed remote. Still, Pete would collect her if he was first home. Would she have time to return to O'Neill's either and purchase the sandals she'd seen in their window? She glanced at her watch again and hoped so, and that they remained open 'til six. Yes, she'd buy them as a gift to herself to celebrate their anniversary; that would please Pete too, who chided her for not thinking of herself more. The cream pair that were comfortable and flat, but not so old-fashioned that Grace would mock her.

The elderly couple now at the box were ever so slow, simply couldn't agree as to what seats they wanted.

'No, thank you, far too near the stage.'

'And an aisle seat, please.' The husband gestured towards his feet. 'Long legs. No, not the balcony, my wife can no longer manage the stairs.'

'If we might have the seats we usually book, row J, and

to the right.'

'Sorry, but I'm afraid they're already booked.' The assistant lifted the ringing phone as she spoke and a lengthy conversation followed. 'Row L, I can give you that.'

They both reluctantly agreed.

Rose booked quickly, grasped her tickets with relief and made her way onto the street outside. She walked swiftly from the theatre, and towards Talbot Street where she had parked her car. A loud noise that sounded like a car backfiring, but louder, made her pause. 'Whatever is that?' she wondered, as a voice from nearby shouted, 'It's a car bomb.'

Rose halted at the corner and paused, disbelieving. Gazed down Talbot Street, as it stretched before her down to the traffic junction where it intersected with Gardiner Street. A busy shopping street, packed with commuters from a youthful workforce who walked briskly towards Connolly station to take their trains home. Even more crowded than usual because of the bus strike. But instead of walking swiftly away from her, a mass of people surged forward in her direction, several of whom stood out in stark form and were imprinted on her brain.

A girl, no more than nineteen, in a floral summer dress, dragged forward by a youth, her stiletto-heeled shoes hand-held as he she struggled, barefoot, to keep up with him.

A mother, who paused to lift a wailing child from its pram as the crowd pressed all around them unthinking then carried the upturned pram forward with them.

An elderly man who fell to the ground; the three youths who circled his tired body helped him to his feet, then half dragged, half carried him aloft.

And the woman who hit against her as she pushed past, so close that she could see the terror in her eyes and hear her strangled sobs.

They fled a car that blazed behind them and to the left of the street, its bombed-out iron frame black against the yellow flames that raged around it while sprays of orange and red sparks rose skywards accompanied by the bullet-like sounds of shattering glass. She saw the familiar red and white sign for Guineys appear then disappear again into the blaze, as did an ad for eye tests at a discount price, an offer of bed and breakfast, still painted a snowy white, and the sound of more crashing glass, this time from O'Neill's shoe shop window.

Rose found herself pushed tight against the wall. 'I need to get to my car.' She pushed forward but the stampede threw her back against the wall as it continued to steam up the street.

A middle-aged woman who clung to two heavy shopping bags; they slowed her yet her face expressed a determination not to let them go.

A lost child who wailed, and, as his cry pierced the stampede, a youth in drainpipe denims and a leather jacket lifted and hoisted him on his shoulders, from where he looked around in silenced amazement, his small hands clinging to that tightly shaved head.

Behind them, the crackling of wood, the crash of falling masonry and giant plumes of black smoke told her that the fire had spread to nearby shops, and when the crowd thinned she saw a commandeered bus, at the end of the street, that had begun to assist some injured who staggered aboard.

Then straight ahead of her, and from Marlborough

Street, she heard the insistent clang of fire engines, and saw their high red-coloured urgency trapped in a street jam packed with commuter cars, with its footpaths on either side crowded by pedestrians. At its sound some walkers moved to cower in doorways, others climbed the steps to the Pro-Cathedral and stood hesitantly there.

To her left, and halfway up the street, a car suddenly pulled out of its traffic lane and mounted the footpath; she saw it plough into a giant refuse bin that spewed rubbish over its bonnet before it ground to a halt. Another car climbed the footpath too, then another. And to her right, that traffic lane yielded too for one car driver chose to turn in through the open gates of the Department of Education, only to be halted by the cars trying to exit there. She heard the driver sit on his horn in helpless fury, as its persistent honk mingled with the clang of fire brigades and the noisy insistence of ambulances and police cars that rushed to the scene. The exiting drivers finally reversed with painful slowness, and, as that first car drove through, it was swiftly followed by several other drivers to allow the emergency services roar by then swing to the left down Talbot Street. Just then the Pro-Cathedral tolled the angelus bell. *The Angel of the Lord declared unto Mary, and she conceived with the Holy Ghost.*

Rose saw her for the first time, the young female whose naked body — her clothes burnt from her — was spreadeagled on the bombed and bloodied street. She saw her clearly, her burnt hair, her staring eyes, her open mouth from which blood poured, her young breasts, the curve of her belly that darkened to her pubic hair, and her arms spread wide in a futile effort to save herself as she was hurled to the pavement. She gazed at her in mesmerised horror, then a speeding ambulance blocked her again from sight, and when it had passed and the dead remains came into view again someone had covered her dead and bloodied nakedness with a newspaper.

A garda pulled a wide crime scene tape along where Rose stood. 'The North has arrived.' He nodded down the street. 'Target civilians. No bomb warning. No notice at all.'

'Should I go to help the ambulance crews?' she asked hesitantly. 'I'm a pharmacist.'

'Go home, love,' he counselled, 'this is no place for young women.'

'My car, that's it over there, can I get to it?'

'Crime scene. No access. Come back for it in a couple of days.'

'What are we to do?'

'Go give blood,' he suggested calmly, 'that's the best you can do right now, there's an urgent call out for that.'

Rose queued. Joined the long line of Dubliners that wound down by the canal to Pelican House, the silver edifice high above whose door hung a giant beaked bird that nurtured its young with its own blood. A youth offered her a cigarette and she shook her head. 'D'you mind?' he asked, and she shook her head again, then watched him silently as he lit up. 'Where were you when they went off?'

'*They?* There was more than one?'

'Three in all.' He nodded to the transistor he held. 'Want to listen? Parnell Street, Leinster Street and Talbot Street.'

'I was in Talbot Street, at the top end.'

'I was near there too,' he nodded, surprised, 'at Butt

Bridge. Heard the noise and thought at first that an overhead train had some sort of problem. Jesus, we're in for it now.'

She listened to the radio reports, which made it all seem distant from her again. For the media coverage of violence had always been that, a chronicle of distant events, not the world news that had occurred almost at her feet just two miles away. Instead far, far distant from her safe life and her small world. The queue moved forward at a swift pace and she rooted in her bag for change as a nearby shop assistant offered drinks and shook her head to payment, then doused her face with the bottled water before she drank from what remained of it.

'Next please.'

'You know your blood group?'

'Yes, O rhesus negative.'

'Universal donor. Great. What we need most right now.'

She lay back on the bed and stretched out her arm then winced as the needle entered her vein; what a fool she felt to resist a mere pin prick after what she'd just seen. The blood flowed slowly from her arm, down into the narrow plastic tube and from there into the large bag that hung below it. The bag filled steadily as the blood level rose and the dark red liquid inside it measured a quarter pint, then a half pint, then three quarters and finally a pint, then the phlebotomist withdrew the needle and covered her arm's tiny cut with cotton wool that she sealed with a plaster. 'Cup of tea? Come with me.' The small cubicle boasted a desk and a chair and she nodded towards a phone. 'Do you want to call family? Try, you may just get through. All local calls on us.'

Tea came as she dialled Pete's number. 'We regret,' a polite voice told her, 'that due to city centre disruptions, all local numbers are currently inaccessible.' She swore loudly as she banged the receiver. Phones jammed. Panic suddenly gripped her. Had Pete been city centre too? She racked her brain for what he'd told her of his work schedule that morning but couldn't remember it from a myriad of other mornings when he'd told her that he had meetings at ... and Ann, if he had been in the city, who then had collected her? She frantically dialled the crèche. 'We regret ...' the polite voice spoke again ... 'that due to city centre disruptions ...'

'Can get you some biscuits if you like. Chocolate. Keep up your energy.'

'No, but thanks for the tea.'

'You ready to go then? Look, if you can, it's best you walk 'til you're well clear of the city. You well enough to do that? Traffic's chaotic ... airport, sea ports, roads north and train stations all sealed. They'll get them,' her eyes filled with angry tears, 'and when they do I hope they swing.'

'At last.' Pete dragged her inside. 'Am I glad to see you. Thank Christ you're safe.' He held her, but she felt nothing save for her feet that ached.

'How's Ann?' she asked as she pulled off her shoes.

'Fine, she kept asking for you, took forever to get to sleep. Don't wake her,' he called as she went to go upstairs, 'she's fine, honest. Where were you when the bombs went off?'

'All I feel now is how much my feet ache, and how I hate myself,' she threw her shoe from her, 'as if that matters.'

'Have you eaten?' he asked calmly, changing the subject.

'No. But if you want to help, just make me that Irish cure-all, a cup of strong tea.'

'Why can't you tell me?'

'Because I don't want to remember,' she almost shouted.

'Ann brought you home a drawing she made,' he said after a time as he placed a tray before her. 'Look like a rainbow to you?' He smiled. 'All the colours there anyway. I read her story which eventually got her to sleep.'

'Her godmother says that she much prefers sums. D'you think Grace is OK?' she asked, suddenly alarmed again. 'I'll try and phone her.'

'All phones are still out. Eat, Rose. Please.'

'I can't.'

'Better that you do. Please, for me.'

'I'm OK. I'll cope, honest. I always felt safe here 'til now, that's all. Dublin was my home, my favourite place. I loved it. Safe? After this? Anyway, I suppose we just got to get on with it. What's to be done? The washing? I could run the whites cycle, I suppose.'

'That can wait too.'

'No. I'm better to keep busy.' She left him and went outside to their small garden where the baby clothes hung, unpegged each item then came back inside and folded them neatly. 'Have to shop for groceries tomorrow too, make a list now, anything special you want?'

'Rose. Please.'

Once in bed she slept fitfully, then woke later as Pete slept on. She moved closer to him, spooned her numbed body around his, felt his round buttocks soft in the hollow of her pelvis then raised her hand to his chest and felt the steady pounding of his heart. For a fleeting second she hoped she could forget and be eager again for the comfort she found with his body and their warm need for each other. But no, she still just felt numb. She closed her eyes and tried to match the rhythm of her breath to his. What time was it? Three ten. Now three twenty. And then three twenty-five, the full moon high outside as she got up and made her way to their daughter's nursery. Ann lay there quietly as her small chest rose and fell in silent sleep. A suddenly ferocious need to protect her daughter swept through her. But how? For so much work had gone into her making.

She remembered again her first sight of that tiny blood-streaked body, then heard with joyous relief that piercing first cry that assured her her newborn lived. And what a myriad of milestones they'd shared since then. The first morning Ann had sat up alone, how she'd raced to call Pete to come quickly; the first evening she'd crawled, he'd been home to see that, and how they'd all cheered her when she'd first hauled herself upwards and stood upright, clapped her and called that she do it again. After several fretful nights, that first tooth that had finally appeared, with her first birthday shortly after. And what a fuss Pete had made for her to blow out her one candle.

She'd been so brave before the vaccinations needle, and how foolishly safe Rose had believed she'd been, free from the horror of childhood death, what a naïve fool she had been. And so much work had gone into her making. Yes all of that, and so much more. For what? A bloodied and naked body spreadeagled on a street and covered by newspaper.

Rose left the room, went downstairs and made tea

again. Well, as a glorious response to mass murder, she told herself, she would make yet another cup of highly sugared tea. Yet as she plugged in the kettle in fury a dragging pain pulled from the pit of her belly and told her that soon she would menstruate, would bleed. She placed her hand down between her thighs ... yes, red womb blood, yes, fresh red blood. She left the flow stain her clothes and, too weary to care otherwise, she took her teacup, climbed back upstairs and tried yet again to sleep.

Come morning, numbness yielded to rage as she watched the TV coverage, desperate that the Gardaí would get the bombers. Drawn to its destruction in mesmerised horror even as it repelled her. Twelve dead in Talbot Street, eleven of them women, one eight months pregnant, six of them under thirty years of age. To include a French student whose Jewish family had survived the Nazi occupation. Four bombs in all, one too in Monaghan, thirty-three dead, hundreds injured.

'Don't watch it, it won't do you any good.'

'I have to. I need to know that they've got them.'

'Let me hold you for a time.'

'I just desperately need to know they've been caught.'

'OK. I'll look after Ann. Eat, though, you have to eat.'

'Just tea, pour me another if you want to help.'

'You can't live on tea. Here, I'll cook—'

'No, just tea.'

'Got them?' he asked again later.

'No, no arrests yet.'

And as day wore to evening and there was still no news of detentions, she began to wonder about them. 'Where were they now? Safely triumphant somewhere? Had their achievements even enhanced their status in some distant, evil place, affirmed their strength, their power, their maleness? Did they perceive themselves as heroes? And as their deadly destruction was flashed around the globe, watched by millions as she too watched it, did they glory that these deeds had in some way rendered them immortal? Did they believe as Carson, founder of the first loyalist paramilitaries, did, that they might use *all means necessary* to achieve their ends? And if so, would they argue that this, yes this, had been necessary? And as their First World War forebears had marched outwards to butcher fellow Christians and Europeans did they believe that *greater love than this no man hath than to lay down his life for his friends?*

And did those nationalist paramilitaries, doubtless already plotting an equally horrific revenge, believe all that too? Believe as Pearse did, who once claimed that *bloodshed was a cleansing and a sanctifying thing and the nation which regards it as the final horror has lost its manhood.* And as at Easter when they'd occupied the city centre did they believe too that *one man can free a people as one man redeemed the world ... that they stood up before the Gall as Christ hung naked before men on the tree.*

Did they both believe they had an inalienable right to play God and so decide as to who might live and who might die? And if they did, was the blood sacrifice they both, as Christians, instigated any different from that of Christ?

She knew so little of male heroes and their warriors, until suddenly she was back there again. Eleven years of age, twelve, not much more, and she'd just menstruated for the first time and had innocently feared that her own womb blood heralded, not a growing fertility and potential for life's creation, but death. How she'd stood on the school podium as a sea of upturned faces watched her curiously from below. She saw the Classics teacher Miss Behan, once more heard her plimsolls creak as she circled her, felt the cold shears close by her ear, and heard again the loud click as blade met blade. And her knowledgeable voice carried to her, and echoed down the years. 'You will join my final class, Rose Leahy, where we will bid farewell to the ancient cultures of Greece and Rome. For the modernists and industrialists have won, us classicists have lost. And lost too will be the heroic and epic quest of boy to man, man to hero and hero to god and the confrontation he makes with death at each stage and rite of passage.'

But she hadn't taken Behan's courses, she'd taken science instead.

Then it came to her again. That naked body, female as hers, her clothes burnt from her, spreadeagled on the bloodied street. Saw again her burnt hair, her staring eyes, her open mouth from which blood poured, her young breasts, her curved belly that darkened to her pubic hair, her mangled legs. Her arms that she'd spread wide in her futile attempt to save herself as she was hurled to the pavement. And later, what remained of her covered by a newspaper.

Was it heroic, or glorious, or deserving of any eternal memory? No. It was obscene.

Pete held Rose's hand as they left the train at Tara Street and made their way towards Butt Bridge, a spray of white and yellow roses that she had brought heavy on her arm. The Liffey flowed sluggishly beneath the ancient bridge, upstream towards O'Connell Street and downstream past the decrepit dockside buildings and out towards the sea. They passed a lone paper seller by Liberty Hall, where the smiling young faces of the new and needless dead stared out from its front page, while an eerie silence, coupled with the smell of smouldering ruins, still hung over Talbot Street. She tried to pray, but the familiar words faded as dust on her tongue; how could God have allowed it so?

'If you could leave these flowers by O'Neill's shoe shop.'

The garda on duty nodded.

She saw herself then, as if outside herself, stand by that same shop window as she'd peered at the selection of sandals inside on that previous Friday, her interest heightened by the early summer weather. Heard herself consider, as if from some distant place, which sandals might she buy: flat preferably, she didn't care to stagger around in stilettos; maybe the white there ... no, definitely not the red, too daring for her taste; or those cream, yes, why not buy them now, the flat comfortable-looking pair. Rose watched her past self move to enter the shop then saw her pause to glance at her watch, shake her head and move to walk swiftly up the street and away. That girl, that earlier self, separated from her by a mere few days, was she lost forever now? Did an unbridgeable chasm divide them one from the other? And the roses ... she watched as the garda placed them where she had recently stood, but what a pathetic tribute they made to life's loss and its survival.

Pete's voice brought her back with a start as she heard him enquire in his pragmatic way if they might take her car, and then felt his hand firm on her arm as they stooped beneath the cordon and entered the bombed-out street. Hand in hand, past where the street cleaners had piled charred wood and shattered glass into giant heaps, past the burnt-out remains of O'Neill's, past the destroyed Guineys, past the wreck and twisted metal of the car bomb. Past the blood marks, now circled in white chalk, where the human dead had lain. The force of the blast had blown the side windows from her own car, and the flames had covered it in a thick veil of grey ash, and she watched as Pete shook the front seats clean, then nodded that she sit inside.

'No. Passenger seat. I'll drive.' Her husband turned the key in the ignition and adjusted the rear mirror, and as she glanced back, the baby seat, drenched in broken glass, came into view. A low scream rose from the pit of her stomach but she made no sound; instead she heard the first scraping sounds as wipers fought to break the ash dust. In time, the window half clear, he pulled out and drove home.

11

Dublin's bells chimed their slow and mournful dirge as the city's citizens went to their churches to pray for their needless dead. Rose knelt close by Pete on the hard wooden pew, noted that Grace was with the choir, then glanced around that familiar space, her gaze pausing at each shrine before it moved on. To Saint Anthony first, he who ensured the safe arrival of postal mail, then to Saint Francis, who so loved the natural world, then to Jude, patron saint of hopeless cases. And beyond them the shrine of the Virgin Mother, arms outstretched behind her penny candles and May flowers. Separated from each other by the confessionals, their velvet curtains red against dark wood. Had the bombers already asked their Christian God for forgiveness, and had he, their all-merciful father, granted them that? Rose shook her head as she felt Pete take her elbow, then heard his low whisper that she sit, but she shook her head and stood as the celebrant intoned the names of the dead.

Collette Doherty, aged 20, and pregnant
Siobhan Roice, aged 19
Marie Phelan, aged 20
Anne Marren, aged 20
Josie Bradley, aged 21
John Walshe, aged 27
Simone Chetrit, aged 30
Breda Grace, aged 35
Anne Byrne, aged 35
Maureen Shields, aged 46

May McKenna, aged 55
Dorothy Morris, aged 57
Elizabeth Fitzgerald, aged 59
Concepta Dempsey, aged 65.

Thirteen women and one man. All innocent. All dead, dead as statues. She heard the choir chant the *Kyrie*, joined in the faithful's response *Christ have mercy*, then stood for the gospel, her head dizzy with exhaustion. Prayers and responses flowed around her as they followed, as if from a distant place, interspersed with loud shuffling as the congregation knelt once more, then by their silence as the celebrant slowly intoned *This is my Body, This is my blood*. She gripped the front pew, her knuckles white as she saw her again, imprinted, as if carved in blood, in her mind's eye, the dead woman, her body spread eagled on the bombed and bloodied street. Burnt hair, staring eyes, so near that she could read the headlines in that newspaper that cloaked her nakedness. 'Bus strike to continue' it proclaimed in large black capitals, and beneath that report a laughing photo of two young children on a beach: 'Sunny weekend promised'.

'You alright?' Pete's hand covered hers again.

'It's Grace ...'

'Yes. She sings *Stabat Mater*.'

She looked her way and saw, not the Grace she now knew, but a younger friend in her girlish school gymslip, cream blouse and grey and yellow tie, and heard her begin to sing, as if from some lost place, *Bring flowers of the fairest, Bring blossoms the rarest ...*

'If I can sleep tonight,' she began, as they arrived home.

He covered her with a rug as she lay on the sofa, and as

she closed her eyes she heard him move around the kitchen doing the tasks that were usually hers. The sound of water as he filled the kettle, then the loud click as he plugged it in, then a second click as he switched it on. She knew from the sounds that followed that he filled the dishwasher, then was conscious of him tiptoe past her to the garden outside and bring in the clothes. It irked her to know that he wouldn't fold them as she always did, rather throw them on the hot press shelf in an untidy pile. It irked her even more to realise that such trivia still mattered to her.

'Tea? Have this while I scramble some eggs. Will you have bacon too?'

'Thanks. You're good to me.'

'Loving is doing. If I'd seen what you've seen, you'd be good to me.'

'Hope so.'

She ate the tasteless food while he left to collect Ann, then made her way slowly upstairs to bed.

'Hear my night prayers,' their daughter demanded as she climbed up beside her.

'Mam's tired, just kiss her goodnight then I'll read your story.' She heard her querulous demands as they left her, heard her call that she wanted her mother and wept as she heard the soft murmur of his voice as it lulled their daughter to sleep.

'You'll feel a bit better tomorrow, Rose,' he suggested from the door. 'Look, I can sleep on the sofa if you like, don't want to wake you as I come up later.'

'No,' she protested loudly.

'Alright, that's fine, just don't want you waking again.' She needed him, the warm consolation of his live body close to hers, needed to feel his round buttocks spooned close to her belly as her hands circled his body and felt the ongoing thump of his heart.

That closeness sustained her, empowered her enough to continue with the mundane aspects of her life over the days that followed ... her work, her childcare, her house duties, as life, mercifully, continued.

'If you were free to follow your heart, Grace,' Rose suggested tartly, 'then so was Brendan.'

It was Saturday and they'd met for lunch in Grafton Street and Grace ate hungrily while Rose toyed, uninterested, with the food before her.

'Look, I'm not a member of the "nail em to the floor and demand a commitment" school.'

'Well, neither am I,' Rose protested, 'if that's what you suggest. Can we give over?' she asked as she pushed the plate from her. 'I'm in a mess and it's nothing to do with sex.'

'What, then? Tell Auntie Grace.'

'God. I don't believe anymore.'

'Why? 'Cause he's a man?' You haven't joined the feminists, have you? I'm delighted he's a man, much better at loving them than us dames. Poses a problem for the lads, wouldn't you say though, although I haven't thought of it like that before now. Anyway, what has our God done to you? Praise him, praise him, thank you for the music and all that, that's what I say.'

'He shouldn't allow it. The slaughter of innocents. It smacks of Herod.'

'Oh that. I know it was terrible, but ... evil's a human choice, it's a mystery. Come on, Rose, they don't have God on their side, they only think they have. Even Dylan, who can't sing, probably knows that, just makes a cool fortune by pretending he doesn't. I prefer Baez, always have, she's the real deal, the genuine article, knows all about diamonds and rust too, just as yours truly. I think of God as the muse, the inspiration for all that magnificent and sacred music over centuries. Play *Pia Jesu*. I prefer the Lloyd Webber version myself, but don't tell the purists. Listen, let it soak in to your bones, that'll help you get through.'

'No dice. Doesn't work with number crunchers.'

'Let me try something else then. You've got me through so often, Rose, I'll get you through this one.'

'With mortal men? This one's with God.'

'Come on, follow me. I'll show you how to sing, to rejoice that you're still alive.'

'I can't be that selfish, not after what I saw.'

'But you didn't do it, you're in no way responsible.'

'No, but it nearly was me, and it might have been Ann too. Passion passes, Grace, children last. Or so I thought. One of the dead was heavily pregnant, did you know that? I took Ann's survival so much for granted, was even proud of the role modern science plays in that. Until this.'

'Well, I've learnt too. I pleaded with Brendan in the end. Was prepared to settle for crumbs. And that, I now know, was a mistake.'

'Oh Grace, that isn't you.'

'Well, I'm not young anymore, and I was never beautiful. I agreed he could have his fiancée and all that came with her, just asked that we get together occasionally. Know what? He said no. It was so humiliating. And when I asked why, he said she was chaste and he planned to be faithful. That seemed to matter to him. Can you believe that? After all we'd had together. And when I still pleaded he lost it, shouted that the only pure bits of me were the notes I sing. Says his career demands a bed he goes to for sleep, a peaceful home front, a quiet wife, a few children.'

'Peaceful? With children? He'll learn.'

'I've been so miserable.'

'And you pretended all along that you were fine.'

'I couldn't. He made me promise not to. Didn't want it linked in any way to his work. Then, as I sang *Stabat Mater* I suddenly knew there's more pain out there than love's betrayal. Nearly lost my concentration at that, did you notice? But I still think she's a bitch, his little miss pure and her giant solitaire. Anyway, she can have him now, for I've had the best of him. And now I've paid for the coffees, there's something I want to show you, for both of us. Come on.'

They left together and made their way towards the river, Rose struggling to keep up with her friend's swift pace and rapid conversation.

'Handel, you'll like him, he was so human. Swore in four languages, isn't that glorious? I always think that as I reach for a high C. And Swift, the creep, tried to stop him presenting *The Messiah* in what once was a fish market. Believed the Anointed One would never be found in so common, so profane a place. How dim can you get?'

They climbed the steep incline from the Liffey, the stone carvings and high spire of Christchurch's ancient cathedral above and to their right, until Grace paused at the large archway that spanned Fishamble Street and stood beneath it. She ignored the busy shoppers that passed back and forth, as she began to sing *Hallelujah, hallelujah*, nervously at first, then with growing confidence. Rose's embarrassed gaze strayed to people all around them.

Hallelujah. Hallelujah. Some of them pushed past them, while others glanced in Grace's direction, smiled, then walked on. A few paused to listen, and, as their numbers increased, a small group circled them.

'Now,' she called to Rose as she finished, 'tell me you still don't believe in the one that inspired that.'

The group applauded. Rose clapped politely and smiled too, but she knew deep down within her that she no longer did so, as if the great composer's message had somehow severed from its roots.

And so, one sunny day shortly after, as she sat on a low bench beneath the blood thorn tree where she and Pete had first declared their love, she killed him, killed the god of her childhood years, the loving and compassionate god who she'd once believed had personally cared for her, the god who'd mapped out her life and who would judge her when she died as to the good and harm she'd done. Killed the omnipotent being for whom she'd believed the very hairs on her head were numbered, and for whom not a sparrow fell to the ground without his knowing of it. Killed him with the cerebral precision of the scientific tools with which she was now well equipped. Killed the god whose pacifist son had allowed militants to subsume his blood sacrifice and make it theirs, the creator who permitted Christian war heroes to kill other Christians, kill Muslim, kill Jew. Their scribes and Pharisees they might always have with them, their Pilots and Herods too, but they would no longer have her. She had lived, fourteen had died by no more than what, a throw of the dice? And suddenly she was back there again outside O'Neill's shop window, beside her past self, that alien stranger who had focused on the cream pair that were both comfortable and flat, then glanced to her watch, shook her head and hurried on.

Was she to find some divine intervention in merely that? How that elderly couple in the ticket queue had irked her.

'No, thank you, far too near the stage.'

'An aisle seat, please. Long legs. No, not the balcony, my wife can no longer manage the stairs.'

'If we might have the seats we usually book, row J and to the right.'

'Sorry, but I'm afraid they're already booked.'

Was she to believe that they, that tiresome pair, had saved her? And if so, why had she lived when fourteen others, a mere few yards from where she'd stood, died? Because they were in the wrong place at the wrong time with the tolerant acceptance of a sadistic God? Or by mere chance? She'd believed God didn't play dice, but did he? Suddenly she was less sure. For he had. And with innocent lives. So he did. She didn't like him one bit, her new God of chance. How she railed at her youthful stupidity. How could she have once believed in his supposed compassionate wisdom, and in the humble but designated role he'd chosen for her to play? A God to whom she personally mattered. He was dead now within her. And she would live on. Without him. Without her personal God. Without his divine plan for her life and without his afterlife either.

'I'd also like the little one from pharmacy there.'

When Rose first read the invitation to Mr Wyndham's retirement party, she threw it aside; then recalling how the elderly consultant had treated her with unfailing courtesy, she rescued it, sent off a pound towards his presentation, and accepted. As the evening approached and it emerged that few of her contemporaries had been included, she was sufficiently flattered to shrug off the inevitable social encounter with Brendan it would entail. So, come Friday evening, she made her way upstairs to the large boardroom, then, as the party was well under way, paused at the door as the low murmur of voices, occasional laugh, and the clink of glasses wafted towards her. Damn. She glanced down at her white coat and realised too late that she might have changed, for the female guests were high-heeled and gowned in summer silks, as they circulated and greeted each other with incredulous delight, cheek against cheek, and smacked the over-shoulder air with loud lipstick kisses. She tread her way gingerly through the crowd to the long table where, beneath the benign portrait of Lord Aynesbury, the hospital's long-dead benefactor, wines, minerals and cocktail titbits were on offer.

'Rose. Nice to see you here. What would you like?'

'A mineral, thanks.'

'Soda water? Tonic? White lemonade?'

'Tonic's just fine.' She helped herself to a cocktail sausage, a smoked salmon square and a crisp cheese and biscuit, all of which she balanced precariously on a small plate, then glanced around for Mr Wyndham. He stood to the side of the crowd; she presumed that the small white-haired woman who sat beside him was his wife. Just then Brendan's fiancée touched the older woman's arm lightly and her diamond sparkled.

'Can I have your attention?' Brendan called loudly and everyone looked his way save Rose, who twiddled the stick that pierced the lemon slice and noticed that the paper umbrella atop it had wilted and now drooped damply over the melting ice cubes.

'We are indebted,' Brendan's voice filled the suddenly silent room, 'to Mr Wyndham, our eminent consultant, who has served this hospital over many decades.'

Several people began to clap and he held up his hand to halt them. 'We all recall,' he continued, 'his endless generosity, particularly to his public patients. I think I can confidently say that in his early years no patient who might have benefited from Mr Wyndham's charitable expertise, no matter how impoverished, was ever refused by him.'

The clapping began again and he raised his hand once more for silence. 'And, in more recent times, I particularly recall his commitment to the eradication of tuberculosis from which his own son tragically died at the young age of twenty-three.'

Rose took a sharp intake of breath. Why had he brought that up, and on what was seen as a social occasion? Trust Brendan to go over the top and put his foot in it. She risked a glance towards the consultant with whom she had worked for so many years. How little she knew of his personal pain or he of hers. Or his wife's, who sat beside him and quietly lowered her head. 'He was unflinching,' Brendan continued, 'in his determination that the new tubercular drugs be made available to all, and gave his full support to the school vaccination programme that has now gone close to eradicating this scourge from our country. And,' he smiled towards the retiree, 'as he has particularly requested that I be brief, I would like you all now to join me in a toast, as we wish him well for his future years.'

Rose raised her glass, then sipped. The ice cubes had melted and the tonic tasted like water.

'I will now call on my beautiful fiancée,' he smiled towards her, 'to present him with this Waterford crystal table piece as a small token of our appreciation.'

Rose watched as she lifted the heavy memento nervously and handed it over, then saw him pass it immediately to his wife. He cleared his throat before he responded.

'Thank you for your fine gesture and good wishes,' he began, 'and I will be mercifully brief.'

Everyone smiled and a few clapped. 'I have been asked,' he continued, 'on more than a few occasions as to what I might do on retirement. My wife,' he nodded towards her, 'may part with some of her beloved garden and permit me to grow some vegetables there. We have, I believe, far too many flower beds,' he smiled down at her, 'don't we, dear? Doubtless I will also be coaxed to visit our daughter in Manchester more frequently and to enjoy our two granddaughters who live there. I may of course escape occasionally to my beloved Wicklow hills for some peace and quiet. And yes, for those of you who've asked, I will still chair the hospital's charity committee; I have, I must protest, been cajoled into doing just that, but only for a further year. Now, perhaps you will join me in a toast to Saint Mary's and to its future.'

'To Saint Mary's,' Rose intoned, raised her glass and sipped. The ice had long melted and what remained of the tonic tasted tepid. The crowd moved to regroup as some queued to wish the retiree well. She suddenly felt hungry too and ate from what was on her plate: cold sausage, dried smoke salmon and melted cheese.

'Oh, hi.' Brendan's mouth was half full of food as he touched her arm.

'N-nice speech,' she stammered.

'Thanks.'

'One of the old school. We shall not look upon his likes again, and all that.'

'Oh come on, he's far from dead yet, just retired.'

'Sees it as a death sentence, I think. Medicine was his life. True, though. On both counts.'

He glanced to his left where his fiancée still chatted to Mrs Wyndham, and a tense silence fell between them.

'How's Grace?' he asked at last.

'Don't,' she began.

'I won't,' he agreed, but his eyes told her differently.

'She's met someone else,' Rose lied.

'Oh.' He waited expectantly to hear more.

'It's hardly a matter for you,' she replied coldly.

'Of course,' he agreed, eyes angry.

'Congratulations on your promotion.' She feigned a bright cocktail smile, determined to change the subject yet also stand her ground.

'Thank you.'

'When do you marry?' she pressed on.

'June.'

'Nice month for a wedding.'

'Mainly women's business.'

They both fell silence then. 'I guess I better go,' she said at last, 'wish him well and all that.'

'Of course.'

'Bye.'

'Good luck for your retirement.' She smiled as she reached the older man.

'Thank you.' He smiled formally. 'And, my dear, you who so generously help in the care of others must also remember to care for yourself.'

She felt her eyes fill with tears. 'Thank you,' she whispered, then fled.

'... and his son had died of TB,' she continued, as she talked with Pete later that evening.

'The great healer?' he replied in a tired voice. 'We three matter to me, no more.'

'More than that matter to me,' she protested. 'I was so proud of what we'd achieved, happy to be part of all those advances in health too. No more filthy one-room tenements, people have houses now, with water, electricity, heating and indoor loos. And all those terrible illnesses we can now cure. TB, so many younger than you or me died from that; syphilis, that destroyed so many marriages and lives. Few women die in childbirth nowadays either, while all those killer diseases of childhood – measles, diphtheria, pneumonia – can be cured too. We've even got free second-level education now, just think of the difference that's going to make. You know that once, and it seems so long ago now, I truly believed that, with all that, I'd come to live and work in a sort of heavenly place. And nowadays too nearly everyone can afford a family car. Then look what's done with all that. Use those nice family cars to blow each other to pieces.'

'I don't care much about people I don't know, Rose. I'm sorry, but I don't. I can't. I can't care about every goddam person in this city. Why should I, what did they ever do to me? I care though, it's not as if I'm heartless through and through. I care for you and for Ann and for me, that'll do as far as it goes, and that's enough caring for me. The truth is, right now I'm exhausted, and worried about the business. I can't take time out from it endlessly just 'cause you can't cope. I need my energy and time for that. What happens to us three if things go wrong there?'

'We'd just do as we did before, live on what I earn until things improved again. What's wrong with that? I'm not extravagant. We'd get by. Business problems. OK, but at the end of the day no one's dead.'

'Yeah, no one's dead. That's the whole point, isn't it? None of us three.'

'Yeah, I suppose so, we're what matters most to me. I hear you. I'm sorry. I'll try to be more with it at home, I will try.'

'That's my Rose.'

'I still get frightened, though. Wish to God they'd find the creeps who did this, arrest them, bring charges, I'd feel safer again then. Until they do, I fear they could be anyone, anywhere. Sometimes I'm too terrified to walk past a line of parked cars, cross the street instead. See a man walk swiftly away from one of them. Why's he walking so fast? What's in that car? The shady geezer who sits by me on the bus. Who is he? Haven't seen him on this route before. And that bag he's carrying. Large and bulky. What's in it? And the silent one, who sits alone in the darkened cinema, then leaves. What's he left there beside his seat? Is there something in that? I know one thing, I can't go on like this. What you don't understand is the worst fear I have, that they'll get you, get Ann, get me.'

'Did they get you yesterday?'

'No.'

'Or the day before that?'

'No.'

'Well then, can you trust that they won't get you

today?'

'I can try.'

'Funny really,' she confided later, 'tried what you suggested, and you know, it's begun to work. I count back all the days and say, listen, you murderers, you haven't got me today, not yet. Strange really, sometimes each day seems, well, a bit like a gift.'

'I back the probabilities now,' she smiled as they chatted later. 'From what I recall of the life stats, I'm likely to live to be eighty-three, and you to be seventy-seven. Can you believe that? All that living ahead for both of us. Not certain, of course, but probable.'

He squeezed her hand. 'That's my Rose.'

'Just two ordinary lives, no great heroics or anything. Did I tell you I tidied out the drawers in our bedroom last week? And do you know what I found? An oyster shell; do you remember, we shared them on our wedding day? And beside it the band with Ann's name and delivery time from her birth. And our blood thorn, I walked past it with her last evening and it was bright red with a multitude of haw berries.'

Even the small things that still annoyed her seemed a bit lovable then. 'You'll both have to move over, you know. I've just fallen in love with being alive. Can you share me with that, with life?'

12

Grace knew from the start that Paul was married. He made no secret of that, for the only occasions he removed his wedding band was when he wanted to show the pale skin beneath it as proof to his wife of his ongoing fidelity. Grace didn't much care about that, most of the men she encountered were married now anyway. And she'd never once met Paul's wife, who existed in a dull and faded sort of way at the periphery of things as she devoted long hours to chauffeuring their three children across north Wicklow; to and from school, to and from their school grinds, and to and from their pony and sailing classes. In between these marathon treks she golfed (badly) and swam (equally badly); she had only recently mastered a demure breast stroke. But she had claimed one victory, for Paul had long ago capitulated to her belief that weekends were together time for family and so, with that ongoing success under her belt, domestic tranquillity prevailed.

Despite all that, it was widely known in business circles that Grace was Paul's mistress. For the major, Fetherington-Gore, Paul's fellow director and chair, had once loudly voiced his belief, gaze fixed firmly on the adulterer, that one never married one's floozies, one's whores; while the adulterer's PA (more essential to the smooth workings of his business than either wife, mistress or even F-Gore) merely shrugged Grace off as yet another of her boss's 'bits on the side'.

Grace and Paul met twice weekly, where their night together began with a glass of Jameson ten as Paul checked the TV for the day's winners while Grace presented the meal she'd collected at the nearby caterers on her way home. She learnt Paul's favourites over time, filet mignon and a French red, or salmon with lemon sauce served with a chilled Pouilly-Fuissé, both followed by fresh fruit and a good cheeseboard. On occasions they broke open a bottle of champagne, to mark a particularly lucrative win on the nags or to celebrate yet another successful deal sealed by one or other of their business teams. The evening always ended with their love-making, after which Paul, gentleman that he was, remained at Grace's side until she fell asleep, after which he quietly left.

Paul quickly came to use Grace's apartment as his city base, and she smiled indulgently on finding his shaving gear and wash bag in her bathroom, three freshly laundered shirts in her wardrobe, and a tweed jacket she particularly liked in her hall press. Indeed, an impartial observer might have accurately concluded that Paul had, as a prosperous African or a good Muslim, merely found himself a second wife.

'What are we bet?'

Grace had first heard Paul's voice before she'd actually seen him, for he'd stood beside her, the sleeve of his check hound's-tooth visible as he held out a wad of notes to the bookie. 'Don't know yet,' she'd laughed. 'I'm new to this.'

'Always trust beginner's luck myself,' he joked. '*New Dawn* down from eleven to eight, lot of late money on that.'

'I'd prefer an outsider,' Grace smiled, 'prefer to make a decent killing or not win at all.'

'So the lady here likes to play for high stakes, eh? Like the sound of that too.' She sensed him appraise her, brown eyes teasing, for despite his stocky build and balding head his tweed frame radiated a certain excitement that she found infectious. 'You call it,' he grinned.

Grace glanced down the chalked numbers to pause at *Try Again*. That there, twenty to one.'

'Two on *Try Again*, Joe, on the nose.' He handed over an alarming amount of money as she fumbled in her bag for hers. 'Come on,' he grinned, 'we'll go by the track, best watch it from the railings.'

'Thanks, but I'm with a crowd from work. Decided to come to Leopardstown on Stephen's Day and blow our end-of-year bonuses.'

'They'll join us there.' He took her elbow in a masterful way and steered her down the grassy slope. 'Where did you leave them?'

'At the tote, where there was a long queue, thought I'd have more fun with the bookies.'

'How right you were. Here, have a look at the parade ring, find *Try Again*, she's a lovely nut brown. Johnson's riding, he's in yellow, see if you can pick him out.' The binoculars brought a rainbow display of horses and riders into larger focus. 'If he manages the early jumps you just never know. Lined them up yet? No. Hey, give me a look. Another call to the tape, they'll be off any minute now.'

The horses thundered towards them, hooves pounding, nostrils quivering, breaths harsh and foggy in the wintry air.

'Three down at the first, and we're still there. Loose horse to the right, has avoided that. Still there, but only just, come on, my beauty, you can do it, come on, come on.'

Grace winced as the whip came repeatedly down on the velvet brown flank. She saw the horse gather speed then take the two that had forged ahead from the inside. They rode neck and neck then, all three ahead of the pack, jockeys' bums high, the yellow she had backed with the dull green of the favourite and a third in bright blue. 'Have a look, keep him in sight, he's to make a few more jumps.'

'Yeah, he's still there.'

'Come on then, over to the finishing post.'

She struggled to keep up with his fast pace as her high heels sank in the damp grass. Now it was between *Try Again* and the jockey that wore blue. 'He's pulling ahead, he'll win, he'll win.'

'Hey, we did it. He's won. You brought me luck. Come on, know Johnson, must congratulate him.'

'What'd it come home at?' a voice shouted their way.

'At twenty.' He raised her arm. Where are your friends? They join us? Hot toddies on me. Johnson, you're the ticket,' he told the jockey, who grinned down at them. 'Grace here brought me luck.'

'Hi, well done,' she smiled.

'Got to collect our winnings, then find your friends, probably at the bar with everyone else.'

Inside a silver Christmas tree twinkled blue lights as her eyes searched in vain for the work crowd. 'Hot whiskies by two, Jameson ten.'

She cupped the warm glass between her cold hands and smiled at him over the rim. Forties, she imagined, stocky, even corpulent, and while he wasn't yet bald his hair had begun to recede. 'I still don't know your name,' she smiled.

'McKenna. Paul. Friends call me McK.'

'I prefer Paul. Hi Paul, I'm Grace, Grace Donovan.' She raised her glass. 'Happy New Year.'

'You've brought me luck, Grace. I need that in my life.'

'Why not?' she agreed as she took another sip of whiskey.

'Happy New Year, Grace.'

'I can't get away,' she protested when he rang two weeks later. 'You know January, auditors in, work late each evening and weekends.'

'You'll come to Cheltenham then, trip's on me.'

'Thanks, but I can't.'

'Yes you can. Need my lucky charm there to guarantee me winners.'

'I'll pick a few before you leave,' she offered in a conciliatory tone, 'and phone you with them.' And she did.

'Need to buy you dinner,' he offered when he returned. 'Two of yours came in, not half bad. How about the Red Cow, by the Curragh?'

'Look, I will see you,' she agreed impulsively. 'Leopardstown, Paddy's Day, how's that?'

'You're on.'

'Hail Glorious Saint Patrick, we've done it again. What a win, home at twenty five.'

'Come in,' she offered as he pulled in by her apartment. 'Cook you something if you like.'

He pottered around her lounge as she tossed a salad and ran up a chicken fricassee. 'I see you like music,' he called.

'My great love,' she assured him. 'Pour yourself another whiskey, food's ready in a few mos.'

He browsed through her cassette collection as she set the table: linen cloth (Belfast), glasses (Waterford), and cutlery (Newbridge). They ate, he thanked her, made no effort to touch or kiss her as she wondered in a bemused way if he just didn't want her.

Until a thick envelope arrived, one that contained air and opera tickets for Verona in four weeks' time. Verona! How could she possibly say no to that?

Grace knew however that she was no longer young. While Brendan's unexpected and sudden betrayal had severely dented her confidence, her mirror also told of small lines around her eyes, a hint of a second chin (despite all her palm slapping), and farther down her body an undoubted circle of flab where panties met belly.

But Verona! She immediately set to prepare for her weekend away with the same vigour that had brought her such career success. A lengthy mirror examination assured that she wasn't fat, even plump, but that she'd look considerably better if she lost, well, say three quarters of a stone. Cabbage soup and apple, the fashionable diet of the time, lost her five pounds, but a low-fat-only regime left her less weak, though she woke with halitosis so ghastly that she feared no mouth rinse or mints would fully eradicate it. She did lose weight on that, and returned to it again after a weekend grape and spring water detox failed to do anything other than leave her faint and dizzy.

As the weekend drew near, her preparation intensified. She used wax strips to tear the hairs from her legs – they hurt like hell – but she feared the razor she'd returned to when Brendan left might leave tiny stubble and bristles and might dampen Paul's eagerness to have her. New undies, then, (never have a new love in an old love's undies), neither white (too virginal) nor black (had they been just too whorish?), but cream-toned. Yes, three bras in all, with good uplifts, and matching panties trimmed with lace. She toyed with the idea of buying bed-wear. Would Paul prefer her naked or in something that begged to be slowly and erotically removed? She realised with surprise that though they'd talked now over several months, she'd no idea what sexual fantasies he secretly harboured. Should she purchase something see-through, or – it was impossible to know –

did his taste stretch to the Victorian and the pleasures promised beneath voluminous cotton folds?

In the end she settled for cream silk that fell to the floor, ball gown and opera style, then booked a beautician for the day before they left for the airport, a specialist in the field who expressed horror at the damage wrought by her carelessly confident youthful routine, and advocated, nay insisted, that she immediately begin an anti-aging nightly programme to include an eye cream, a cell rejuvenation face cream, a neck cream (necks were always the first to go), and an intense night nourishment lotion, all of which came in tiny and very expensive jars, their merits engraved on them in gold. Her eyebrows posed a major problem too, she was told, surely she knew that her face hung on them, and so they were plucked as they'd never been plucked before.

The beautician then presented Grace with a chart of nail polish colours, and suggested she select from it, then whipped out a similar chart for lipsticks. Grace lay back and had fingers and toes painted scarlet, then waited for the polish to dry vibrant against her sallow skin. And she just must accept their avocado bath oil, it was on special offer and wonderfully relaxing for a leisurely soak, and she particularly recommended that she surround the bath with flickering candles as she bathed. And of course the cocoa butter body lotion, the very latest on the market, with a sample tube of their own silky hand lotion thrown in free of charge. What perfume did Grace use? *L'Air de Temps?* Somewhat girlish for her years, for the stylishly beautiful woman there was only one perfume, *Chanel*. She reluctantly agreed that Grace persist with the day make-up she already wore, but absolutely insisted that she outline her lips with dark pencil before she applied her lipstick, not straight from the tube – heaven forbid, no one who knew anything of cosmetics did that – but with a fine-tipped sable brush.

Her hair she determined to style herself.

She sat in the open-air Italian café and sipped her chilled wine. Behind her, narrow buildings rose high from cobbled streets as their windows cast latticed shadows onto the pavements below. To her left, Verona's giant amphitheatre opened to the sky, its cream and pink marble lustrous in the sun, while close by too, down a nearby alley, was Juliet's house, its famous balcony high above its small courtyard. Grace looked around as one at the epicentre of all she most revered, northwards to Salzburg and Vienna, eastwards to La Scala, Milan, and southwards to Callas's home base at Sirmione.

'I want to be straight with you,' Paul's voice came as from far away, 'as to why I want you in my life.'

'Straight?' she repeated, not heeding, for she'd no wish to hear anything that might break the magic of this place. 'What do you mean by straight?'

'I mean honest. And why? Because once we go into that bedroom together, everything changes. You're not naïve, and neither am I. We both know that.'

'I just know it'll change everything for the better,' she laughed.

'I'm no longer young,' he continued, 'but not old either. Yet old enough to know it's important that we agree a few ground rules first.'

How could he? Talk of rules, of all things, in this incredible place.

'Rule one,' he continued, 'I intend to stay married.'

Grace nodded absently, for she'd little problem with

that, his wife safely locked away in the dungeon of her mind. Why was he worried? She'd no wish to risk his banishment to a bachelor flat in lonely misery amid domestic appliances he couldn't operate. 'Let's go to Juliet's house,' she laughed. 'I just can't wait to stand on the balcony there.'

'More wine.' He replenished her glass. 'I do this once, Grace, play it decent, and I'm doing it for you every bit as much as for me. Rule two, no babies.'

'I never, ever wanted children, honest.'

'You sure? I'm wary of you on that score. What age are you? Mid-thirties? Right at that "now or never" decision time for women. Just don't mess me that way, or risk us messing an innocent kid either. You absolutely sure at never being a mother?'

'Certain. I've a sweet god-daughter, I spoil her rotten. That's enough for me.'

'Final rule, the media. They can say what they like of me in their business pages, not elsewhere. My private life remains private. I stay free of tabloid hacks who chase us up for saleable tittle-tattle. There are venues back in Dublin that we can attend together but others we have to avoid.'

'Paul,' she put down her glass, 'can I ask you something? Is this your idea of foreplay? I came here in the belief that ...'

'OK. Rules over. Romeo, here I come. Lead on, Juliet.'

'The Italian folk tale's different from Shakespeare's version,' she explained as they strolled hand in hand down the narrow alleyway to Juliet's home. 'The bard was a monarchist, so the establishment wins as Romeo's wealthy family refuse to accept Juliet as his impoverished choice. But this is Italy and their version permits romance and passion to win, no one dies and Juliet gets her man.'

'Well, you know the Brits, nation of shopkeepers. Lead

on.'

'O Romeo, Romeo,' she called down to him from the high balcony, 'wherefore art thou, Romeo?'

'Right here, whenever you're ready to jump.'

'Join me, my Romeo, perchance at our siesta time.'

'Now there's an offer I can't refuse.'

They lay together in the shady room and made love until night fell. And it was good.

Grace sat in the open-air amphitheatre and looked to the circular stage below. Tourists and locals mingled and chatted all around her. 'Just flown in from New York,' a nearby voice confessed, 'find Verona kinda small, it's cute, though, yeah, it's cute.' Ten Italian voices rushed in to put him down. 'The Met? He thought they could sing there? They were wooden, and cold,' a woman gestured dramatically towards the nearby mountains, 'more frozen than the highest Dolomite. What did their technical purists know of passion, of love? What did they know, yes, come, come, tell her, yes, yes. You've been to London too? *Si, si,* to Covent Garden? This man here, he goes to London for opera, is he sick in the head? Covent Garden with divas who love with their hats on for he mustn't toss her hair. And to Seville? You were there too? Another New York joke? Spain may have its cigar factory. Ah, at last you come to Verona. For Verdi? For Callas? *Si, si,* the greatest of them all. Callas, ah, *Va Pensiera*. Maria, why did you die so? Alone in a wintry Paris apartment as you yearned for Sirmione; for here, for home.'

The crowd grew suddenly silent as darkness fell, save for a yellow moon that hung low in the sky as it cast a river of light on the stage below them; then Paul lit her *moccoletto* and the performance began. Grace felt his hand move to cover hers as Radames struggled with his secret love for the slave girl Aida and the news that war was inevitable. She glanced at Paul covetously during *Celeste Aida*, noted that his balding forehead had garnered a new sprinkling of freckles, noticed too how his brown eyes widened as he listened. Yet his ruddy cheeks and chin were wondrously smooth, and his shirt opened at his neck to a small triangle that boasted another crop of new freckles. She smiled and knew that she loved him.

Time passed and Paul became a part of Grace's routine, as comfortable as an old shoe and familiar sock. He called to her apartment twice weekly, made it something of his second (city) home, and when they ventured outside together as they did for special occasions to mark her birthday or the anniversary of their first time as lovers it was to dine in small restaurants well off the beaten track. Occasionally their business paths crossed, and while Grace took good care to avoid functions when his wife might be present, when they did so meet he merely nodded to her casually as if to a distant business acquaintance. She missed him most at Christmas, and grew to hate that celebration of birth and family that he spent away from her. Over that time, as she determined to recall their initial meeting on Stephen's Day, his spouse surfaced from the dungeon of her mind and grew present to her as a surprisingly vibrant inner being. Laughed with him as he lifted his youngest to pull red-berried holly boughs, laughed again as their youngest sent his Santa letter chimney high, and mixed Christmas pudding with him, as they vied with each other to add raisins, sultanas, cinnamon and candied peel. Was Grace of little consequence to him compared to this suddenly present woman who shared his name, his children, his home and his wealth? The prospect made her miserable, a misery that not even her favourite carols and their musical celebration of Christmas could assuage.

August too presented its pocket of loneliness, one that lasted throughout that month, as he disappeared off, with family in tow, to the Riviera. And, as many of Grace's clients and staff holidayed over that time too, work offered little distraction from the loneliness she felt inside, only to walk home each evening to her empty apartment through crowds of strange tourists, ever eager for even a brief sight of his so beloved and so familiar face. Once there, she went from room to room and softly caressed what she retained of him: his beloved tweed jacket that still hung in her hall closet, his two white shirts, newly pressed, that hung in her wardrobe (had his wife ironed them?), and the shaving foam that stood amid her soaps and shampoos on the bathroom shelf.

She lifted her phone to call Rose, then realised as it rang and re-rang that Rose holidayed too, in Greece of all places, and hurriedly left a message that she would so like, as god-mother, to take Ann out once they returned.

Ann's five now and at big girls' school. She wears the grey gymslip of Saint Martha's and its cream blouse, with a grey cardigan (when it's cold) and knee-high grey wool socks and black shoes. Her hair is long and tied back in a ponytail with a cream band and bauble to hold it in place. She sits at a round table with five other students and takes down from the blackboard into her copy book.

She likes sums best and can count to nine now, and write the nine numbers into her copy, then add them to one another, one to one which makes two (she sometimes counts on her fingers to get the answer right), and when it's correct she gets a tick in her copy. If her writing is tidy and neat as well she gets a silver star. She never gets a gold star because she still draws her lines crooked under each sum. She especially can add five pence and five pence too to make ten pence for the pocket money Dad gives her each Saturday, five pence to save in her piggy bank and five pence to spend in the nearby sweet shop. She walks to the shop on her own and takes a long time to choose from pink rock bits that are hot and minty, jelly babies that are sugary and sweet, aniseed balls that she can suck for a long time, and dolly mixture that have different tastes and colours. Sometimes she gets change of two pence back and she keeps that to spend on Tuesdays.

At home, Dad helps her to read while Mam cooks their dinner. She uses her finger to trace under the words one by one, then says them. If the words are too long, he tells her to break them up into two or three pieces and say them, and sometimes she copies the hard words down on a page and Dad puts a star beside them then pins the page on the fridge door and they chat together about them. Mam sometimes gives her pudding as well as dinner, apple pie with custard, or cheesecake with cream. On Sundays they have a special dinner that Dad cooks and she likes that best because she gets lemonade to drink instead of just milk.

At the weekend Mam takes her to dance class where she wears her special shoes and learns set dances. For *The Walls of Limerick* she holds hands, moves to and fro to the music then swings round and round which she loves, even when it makes her dizzy. She likes *The Siege of Ennis* too, where everyone dances in a circle for a time. Each Sunday Mam takes her for swimming lessons and she puts on her yellow water wings before she goes into the pool. The water is cold when she first gets into it, and then it gets warmer.

She does the dog's paddle and likes to splash with the others, except when the water gets into her eyes.

Grace teaches her to sing 'All Things Bright and Beautiful' and when they go for a walk she tells her to pick out all the bright and beautiful things she sees all around her. The bright sun in the blue sky, and all the bright rainbow colours as well, the red door, the green bus, even the clouds that are just puffy white. Then she picks out all the beautiful things, like the flowers and the trees. Then she names the great creatures, lions and tigers like she sees in the zoo, and dinosaurs from long ago (even from before Grace was born). She points out the small creatures then, the robin redbreast, the sparrow, the yellow finch and all the other birds. She doesn't understand what 'wise' means, but everything is wonderful because Grace is with her, and they sing her favourite song together.

Grace ran the shower, turned the dial, waited for the water to heat, stepped beneath it then felt the camomile soap soft between her fingers. She soaped her face, decided as she did so that her hair could wait, for she'd wash it later that evening before she left for dinner. Mirabeau. She smiled at the prospect, booked to mark Paul's purchase of his first horse, yet to be named. She'd attend as part of the business crowd, he'd insisted on that, determined she who brought him luck would be there. She smiled at the names he'd suggested as she soaped her body then rinsed the frothy bubbles from her skin. *Lucky* and *Verona*, while she favoured *Bewitched* and *Only You*. Unsure what other names would be suggested, and in the end which one would win.

She ran the water over her breasts and belly, then took the towel that warmed on the railing and wrapped it around her body. She dried her back, then moved to her breasts, hit against something though the mirror told her that her breasts looked the same as always. Body lotion then against her skin: her feet, legs, body, arms and breasts. She paused again, for there was something sinister there, a hard knot of flesh lumped beneath her palm. She touched it again and swallowed, felt the fresh taste of toothpaste and the minty flavour of mouthwash against her throat. Definitely something there. Touched it nervously again with her fingertips, felt the soft flesh that surrounded it move, then shook her head and fastened her bra. Yet the lump remained in her mind, larger now than when she'd first felt it, as if the breast itself was dwarfed by it. Probably nothing, some sort of large spot, a hive or something, no more than that. Or maybe an abscess, though it wasn't at all sore as an infection might be, or just a benign lump that was of no consequence. A lump not much bigger than a pimple was not going to interfere with her evening. Couldn't allow such an irrational fear to spoil Paul's party.

Dress on, face made up, hair coiffured, one last glance in the mirror, and she banged the door on her fears. Yet she knew the name she wanted now. She'd urge Paul to name the new filly *Lucky*.

13

How her lost breast obsessed her. Grace viewed it, covered it, then viewed it again. Disbelieving. As one who had a phantom breast as amputees had phantom legs, the body she now occupied distant from her, as if that mutilated chest belonged to some far-off stranger. She sat up in the bed and gently peeled back her nightdress and looked again to where her left breast once had been. A vivid red gash was all that remained, slashed angrily down her chest to the right of her nipple, with what little of the soft breast that now remained blue-white against the tan line where she'd once had a cleavage. With the white gauze that covered where the lump had been, and where her wound was deeper still.

Yet she was relieved to be home again and free of those visitors she hadn't wanted. She saw them again in her mind's eye as they'd crowded into her hospital room and around her bed. Her boss from work with the wife she'd seldom met, both awkward, as those who'd drawn the short straw: well, someone from work had to visit, hadn't they? Two from the church choir, both younger than her, their pert breasts high under summer shirts, and four from the chorus of the G&R. All arrived together on their way home from work, while she'd behaved as if she hosted a cocktail party, introduced them brightly to each other and urged them to get to know each other as if they had any interest in doing that. And all that time, the wound beneath her nightdress had throbbed and ached and all she'd wanted to do was escape again to sleep. Rose and Pete had visited too; not that he'd wanted to either, rather feared for a wife too upset to drive home alone. So she couldn't really talk to Rose and tell at least one woman how it truly was. And they'd all left her flowers and chocolates. The former wilted and the latter melted, for the control switch for the heating couldn't be lowered as it was for the entire hospital. And cards and written messages that suggested recovery was fun. As if she had the energy to do anything much, least of all that.

She sensed bleakly that her fate didn't matter much to most of them, save for Rose and Paul who'd both come up trumps. Wary of the C word that none dared utter, and their fear of it for themselves. Rose, with her unflinching faith in the power of modern medicine, somehow communicated to her, and Paul knew she was lucky and had no doubt whatever that her luck would hold.

'It throbs,' she'd confessed to Paul.

'You've painkillers for that. I'll get you water to swallow them.'

It irritated her to hear him rattle around her kitchen, open press doors then close them again; surely he knew by now where the glasses were stored. 'Press to the left,' she called, 'left of the hob.' Then the welcome sound as tap water flowed.

'Pills are in the drawer there.' She watched him fumble in the dim light. 'Take care you find the right ones.'

'These here, look. Drink them down with this.'

She swallowed, felt the pill stick in her throat briefly, then swallowed again. 'Takes ten minutes or so, then it'll ease a bit.'

'Good, then you can sleep.'

'Want to see it? My war wound?'

'Not particularly.'

'Alright. Another time. Look, you better get some sleep too, you've to work tomorrow.'

'And you?'

'Home care team will call. I'll be alright. Wish I could just sleep but it throbs all the time.'

'Even after the painkillers?'

'Uh-huh. They just dull it a bit. Hold my hand.'

'Sure thing.'

'I love you.'

'My lucky charm.'

'You said I brought you beginner's luck. Beginner too at this.'

'Worst over now. The rest will be easier.'

'Well, maybe.' Look, the sofa's not much for sleeping on, want to get in here beside me?'

'You're sure?'

'Yes. I need you.'

'Alright. Won't touch you there, honest.'

They clung to separate sides of the bed, a wide and empty space between them where his outstretched hand met hers. She tossed restlessly and feigned sleep until she finally heard his breath grow slower and steadier and they both finally slumbered.

She felt rested when she woke. She opened her eyes to an empty bed and sounds from the kitchen. He brought her juice and toast, with a mug of strong coffee.

'Only for wives. Maybe I've two for a while.'

She watched as he shaved, through the open bathroom door, his face familiar in the mirror that she could clearly see from the bed. In his old-fashioned way, cheek and chin thick with white foam. She heard the steady scrape of his razor as he drew it through the soap, left cheek, right cheek, chin, then the small space between lip and nostril, more carefully there, followed by a splash of water. He turned to face her, towelled from his midriff down, then patted his face dry with a second towel and looked at her expectantly.

'Home care team arrive at ten. I'll survive.'

'Rose ordered food, dinner's in the freezer. Use the walking frame when you're out of bed, just in case, you may still be weaker than you think.'

The door banged and she was alone.

Chemo. When the infusion needle had drip, dripped its medicines into her veins, she'd grown a habit of peeling back the plaster that covered the wound it made to peer nervously beneath the gauze for signs of infection. Clean wound. Relief, nothing to fear there. Yet how sick it made her as she bent over the bed and retched again, and while her stomach heaved dryly no vomit came. She felt the sick rise to the back of her throat once more, heard it gurgle there, tasted its vileness, then swallowed it back down. To heave and retch again, and repeat that pattern, her forehead damp with sweat. If only she could vomit and be done with it. She lifted the basin, set it on her belly before her and waited. No vomit, though she still felt nauseous and ill.

The cancer sales lady called as arranged. She brought aids, assured her she understood, and ignored the giant basin that wobbled on her belly.

'Wigs? Your own hair colour, I presume?' She was heavily made up herself, hair so sealed with hairspray that it looked almost like a wig itself. And she smiled an eager smile at Grace then lined three of her offerings up on the dressing table. 'This, perhaps?' She lifted the first one. 'Let me put it on.'

Grace felt it cling to her head, tight as a swimming cap, as she resented the alien fingers that pushed tight into her scalp and settled what was left of her own hair beneath it. 'See,' she handed her a mirror, 'just as your own.' She smiled brightly. 'No one will know.'

'It's uncomfortable.'

'Or perhaps?' she offered with a bright sales smile, 'you might prefer a slight change of style. We don't recommend any radical change, invites comments,' she added sotto voce, 'and we don't want that now, do we?'

'It's very uncomfortable.'

'It is?' She sounded surprised. 'Only for a short time. You'll soon get used to it. Don't sleep in it, of course, only for daywear. Happy?'

'Let me think about it.' The mirror assured Grace that she looked better, more as she always had. Better than with her thinned hair that grew finer as each day passed and her white scalp that became even more visible still.

'Decided? Good. And now for your breast.' Four shapes, which do you think matches the good breast best? It's nestled, you see, into this lace-trimmed cup. We have other styles too, if you prefer. See, it's hidden away. Your secret.' She smiled her sales smile again. 'For none but you to know.'

'I think I'm going to be sick again.'

'I can offer you some bandanas too.' She gestured in a practical way towards the basin. 'Cover the baldness if you want a rest from the wig.'

'Thank you.' She nodded bleakly towards the display

before her. 'Can you let yourself out?'

'Of course.'

Grace felt her restrained hand on her arm as she attempted to rise from the bed, as she smiled her goodbyes, then heard the hall door shut. Tiredness returned, that numbed feeling that soaked into every part of her being and permeated her bones as she lay back and attempted to sleep once more.

When she woke it was evening and she hobbled with the walking frame to the window and looked outside. Below her, the river meandered along between wide footpaths jammed with pedestrians and streets chock-full of traffic. Bright neons flashed their sales messages from nearby signs, and beyond them, glamorously dressed women and their beaus made their way to restaurants and the theatre, while she … All of the city below her seemed so vibrant, so alive, as if everything there, animate and inanimate, was suffused with life: the very stone footpaths breathed, the sluggish river waters, the swans and moorhens that swam there, even the modern glass and stone buildings and the mass of people who passed beneath them. And it seemed to her then that all of that animation, and the life she'd shared with them, was slowly ebbing away from her.

'We'll try radiation too, throw everything at it, give it all we've got.'

'Dear, God,' she pleaded, 'just let me live.'

Ann lies on the kitchen floor, paper and paints before her as she makes a card to send Grace. She wears her school uniform, her grey gymslip and cream shirt from Saint Martha's, with her hair loose because Mam has washed it and it's still wet. The fringe that's too long drips into her eyes and she pushes it back and begins. Grace is sick, as she was once with her sore ear, and she wants to tell her to get better.

So she folds the white sheet of paper over, makes a crease down the middle, then takes care that the corners match at each side. Mam has lined up the stencils with her message and it reads 'Get Well Soon' in big capitals. The stencil has only one 'o' for 'soon' and she knows she must remember to use it twice to spell 'soon' right. She traces the 'G' first, then pauses to decide which colour to paint it. 'Red.' She is careful not to spill the water and to stay inside the pencil lines. She traces the 'E' then, and paints it yellow, and after that the 'T' that she paints blue. Mam cooks the dinner and talks to her as she works, then comes over to see how she's doing and helps her to do the next line. She paints 'Well' then, all in green, and traces 'soon' with two 'os' to spell it right, and paints that purple. When it's dry she writes 'Love from Ann' on the inside, with two 'XXs' for kisses beside it, then adds a silver star that she sticks on with glue. Mam takes it to give to Grace.

'Oh, Rose. From Ann? How sweet. Put it there, right beside the bed, where I can see it.'

'I brought food too, Grace, dinners from the deli. I'll heat you something now, put the rest in the freezer.'

'Thanks, but I'm not hungry.'

'You've got to eat, keep up your energy. There's salmon and—'

'I can't taste much anymore. Everything's a bit like sawdust to me. Or smell either. Does the apartment smell OK? I've vomited so often I fear it smells the place for everyone.'

'Stop worrying about that sort of thing. What'll you have?'

'Milk. Like a baby. And heat it a bit. I never believed I'd like warm milk but if anything cold hits my stomach it comes back up.'

'And some fish, you'll coax yourself.'

'Sit with me while it heats.'

'Sure thing.'

'Rose, I need to say something that I think you might understand. I'm frightened, I'm terrified of dying. Oh I know I play cheerful betimes, face made up, nice wig, slash of lipstick, put on my usual brave face, when beneath it I'm—'

'Come on. I'd look at you and say, "Grace Donovan? Now there's a patient who's well on the way to recovery." Here, I'll get the dinner. Want to get up or have it in bed?'

'Help me out. Even if life's a bit loveless now and then …'

'How can you suggest that?' Rose asked as she helped her to the table. 'I'm here, and Paul's come up trumps too.'

'Paul won't last,' she smiles bleakly, 'my men never do for long. He'll stay until I recover alright, or until I die, if that's to happen soon. Why? 'Cause he's the decent sort. He's even decent for horses when they lose him a pile. It's OK, Rose, I'm alright around that now, I just want to live. Life may offer a few more betrayals, but I still want to live it. And right now I pray and strike bargains with God. "God," I say, "just let me recover. And what do you want in return? What price my life?"'

'And what does your God say?' Rose asked nervously as she nibbled her dinner.

'Why would I tell you that?' Grace asked, 'when you no

longer believe in him? You think I'm a bit mad to talk to him? See me as three sheets to the wind to have long conversations with my non-existent fantasy man? Believe he's just another of my once-perfect lovers?'

'I bumped into Brendan earlier today,' Rose rejoined quickly, eager to change the subject. 'He was at the case conference as your file was reviewed. He's pleased with the decision to proceed with the radiation, thinks it's the right one.'

'What will that mean for me?'

'Gives you every chance, Grace. He's gunning for your recovery too, honest.'

'I can just see him, bullying them all as usual. This fish is nice. Thanks. I'll eat something after all.'

'After he came over to me and said, "Grace? Gets to you, does it? Gets to me too."'

'I loved him. What a waste. And God believes I should forgive him. Be truly Christian in that way. Make peace with all my past lovers. Should I? Line them all up and assure each one that, even for a short time, they were each just ever so perfect. Almost God-like. As perfect to me as my all-perfect and loving God.'

'Agree to the radiation,' Rose suggested, surprised that her voice sounded a good deal calmer than she felt inside. 'Brendan has some hope, and so have I, that it'll do the trick.'

'And God. What if he's not there? What if there's nothing? Another betrayal. It was always like that, at the end of every single affair.'

'You never lost hope, Grace, and you're not going to change now. Hope, that's what got you through.'

Grace's skin itched, particularly in the soft fold where her remaining breast met her chest. She scratched it angrily, not caring that she shouldn't, in hatred of the black ink markings of the radiation points. Branded. As some medieval slave. Cancer here. Cancer here. Cancer here. Her nails tore at the itchy parts until the skin broke and wept with her, then grew infected and oozed pus.

The home care nurse tut-tutted. 'Just look at what you've done.'

'Am I dying?' she whimpered.

'No, we trust you'll recover.' Her averted gaze told Grace that she lied.

'So I'm going to die? I'm dying, and I'm not even forty yet.'

The antiseptic she applied stung. 'Doing our best for you, Grace,' she retorted calmly as she covered it with gauze. 'I know it's difficult for you, but try to leave this alone.'

'I'm never going to recover, am I?'

'You may well do. We all hope so. Do you meditate?'

'No.'

'You could try it. Help calm your rage. And there's a hospital support group, one afternoon a week ...'

'I'm not a groupie,' she shouted. 'Anyway, it's not the sort of group I'd ever want to join.'

'Alright.' The nurse patted her blanket calmly. 'Some patients find it helpful, that's all.'

'I do pray.' She nodded contritely. 'Sorry, I know none of this is your fault.'

'That's fine, I understand. Pray if it helps. I can ask the hospital chaplain to visit if you want, bring you communion ...'

'So I *am* dying and you want a priest to give me extreme unction.'

'The sacrament of the sick, only if it would help.'

'None of this is my fault.'

'No one suggests that it is. Pray if that helps you. Grace, love, it's whatever gets you through.'

She felt calmer after and resolved to stay in control, devised a small routine that gave structure to the day. Come morning she clasped the walking frame, her damp hands fearful on its cold metal as she made her slow way to the kitchen. Eggs, yes there were some to the back of the fridge; she'd poach them. When the egg carton shattered to the floor and the yellow yokes spewed in slippery rawness she refused to rage but wept instead in helpless despair at her inability to carry out such a simple task. One egg intact, would she risk to bend down and reach it? She lowered herself nervously, grasped the damp shell, then held it triumphantly aloft. Life comprised a myriad of such small victories now. To wash herself, she could still do that, and brush her teeth, even comb what remained of her thinning hair, and apply body lotion to those dry patches of skin, even dress, if you could call it that, in a fresh nightgown daily. Medicines then, careful to take the correct amounts, and then to pray.

She pleaded for the intercession of the Virgin Mother, recalled her church icon, arms outstretched lovingly, her summer altar bedecked with colourful flowers. *Remember oh most holy Virgin Mary,* she pleaded, *that never was it known that any who sought thy help or pleaded for thy intercession was left unaided* ... *Hail Mary, Holy Mary* as she fingered her rosary, the pearl beads hard beneath her fingers, *Salve*

Regina, Mater Misericordiae, to thee do we cry poor banished children of Eve ... At other times she selected carefully from her library of cassettes and played music, arias of the love she'd yearned for, *Celeste Aida*, *I Have Dreamed*, Verdi's *Chorus of the Hebrew Slaves*, then lay back as the sounds wafted over her. Time passed in that way.

She tried to dial the number yet again. 'Nine.' The dial whirred around, but her fingers, too weak to hold it, saw it whirr back again. 'Nine,' she tried again. Fear made her vomit, then cling to the cord as it fell to a large pool on the floor below her. Again. 'Nine.' One nine dialled. At last. And again. 'Nine.' Hands clammy with fear. 'Nine,' again. To ring. At last.

'Give me your name and full address,' a voice said.

'Grace Donovan. I'm ...' the receiver fell from her hand.

'Keep calm, Grace, and just tell me where you are.' The voice rose eerily from the receiver that dangled down the bedside. 'Trace it,' she heard it say firmly. 'I want a tracer on this straight away.'

She struggled to reach the receiver, felt the congealed vomit slippery in her hand as it fell away again. Tried again, drew it towards her, until it lay exhausted on the bed beside her. 'Hello?' her voice a hoarse whisper. 'Hello? Can you get me help?'

'On our way.'

Her feet were cold, so terribly cold, as were her hands, and she felt the cold climb up her legs and arms. Music faded as shadowy figures surrounded her.

'Hold me,' she whimpered.

A stranger did.

14

'Dead on admission.' The voice spoke with the false sympathy of one for whom such an event was a frequent occurrence.

'When?' Rose asked, hand clammy on the receiver.

'Lunch hour. Let me see, certified at, yes, thirteen forty two. She phoned for an ambulance, they rushed her here, but ... Oh you knew her, you were old friends, I'm sorry. Come down, can you, as you've been listed as a contact person, no immediate next of kin.'

She pushed away the file she'd been reading as Grace's face floated before her as she'd last seen her. Rainbow-coloured chiffon scarf worn bandana-style to cover her bald head, breasts pert beneath her cream nightdress, silicon indistinguishable from flesh. Lipstick held in her right hand, oval mirror in her left. She'd smiled as she'd applied that familiar red slash across her lips. 'Always feel better with lipstick. When I heard the door,' she'd confided, 'I thought it was Paul. Still, it's good to see you.'

Had they phoned him? Hardly, in the circumstances. She must do that, well, not just yet. Needs space to allow it sink in. 'Grace is dead,' she said slowly, and her own voice echoed its truth back across her busy desk. Hadn't sensed her passing, hadn't in any way known. What inane thought, trivial concern or fleeting emotion had distracted that her? What could possibly have been more significant than that? And suddenly she was there again, as she walked along the seafront, then took the sharp left turn down the east pier. Past where the first of the summer strawberries were for sale. Would she buy? Enjoy their delicious fresh flavour doused in thick cream? Had that truly mattered? And then she'd paused at the bandstand, they'd played, what was it, Verdi, yes, the *Chorus of the Hebrew Slaves*. While Grace had struggled for those few last breaths, had fought, all alone to live on. A thousand signs of the truth she'd refused to face flooded her mind. The bio-chemist, that slight shake of her head followed by that downward gaze: 'Not too good, I'm afraid'; and the oncologist's 'There are some, some few indications with which I'm less than happy'; and Brendan's hand briefly on her shoulder: 'We can always hope … remissions, miracles, call them what you will, do, if infrequently, occur.' Even Pete: 'Maybe you should face it, Rose …' She lifted the phone and dialled his number. Engaged. Pessimists all, how summarily she'd dismissed them, trusted instead in her friend's false cheer. 'And Paul has offered to bring me to, guess where, Paris. Now, what one-tit wonder could say no to that?'

She approached the low table through the chilly mortuary air. Grace lay there, eyes closed as if in sleep, except that her face was unusually pale. Rose stretched out her hand and touched her cheek nervously, but it made no movement in return. 'Grace,' she said in quiet disbelief, but there was no reply. She searched for her hand beneath the thin sheet, felt its fingers stiff in her palm and knew that she was dead.

'How should we lay her out?' the attendant asked timidly. 'If you want we can provide a blue shroud.' She nodded towards the nearby press. 'Most prefer to supply their own. Don't get upset, it's just there are a lot of arrangements to be made, and soon. Do you have a key to her apartment? You might find something suitable there.'

'I could buy something,' Rose suggested on impulse, then glanced towards the closed door that promised a hoped-for escape.

'Would you talk with the undertaker and chaplain before you leave?'

'You think I should?'

'Yes, help us move along the arrangements.'

The undertaker wore a heavy suit despite the summer day, a black tie tightly knotted over his starched white shirt, as his firm handshake suggested a clinical concern. She sensed him swiftly appraise her, then suggest a mid-priced coffin with a brass plate that told Grace's name with the date of her birth and the time of her death. No, she didn't think the deceased would want a cross as well, Grace had never understood her life in that way. Did she want brass handles? No. He seemed surprised, then quietly insisted that almost everyone had those so she wearily concurred with that suggestion. And she finally agreed, if from a frozen place inside her, that cream satin lining would be preferable to white or blue, and that the coffin might remain open until the church removal, for there was nothing at all to hide.

Cars? How many did she want for the chief mourners? She stated firmly and swiftly that she didn't want any. And the matter of the grave, he pressed on. Yes, he appreciated all this was distressing for her, but it would help greatly if she knew of a family grave. Was there one? In Dublin? Or outside the city? She had no knowledge of that. Donovan? South Dublin? He'd try Deansgrange, if not there he needed her signature that they might open a new grave. Of course. She signed the page he produced in a half-dazed way.

And flowers? He'd recommend ... well, for youthful deaths, the families usually favoured a spray. He waited quietly as she decided. Yes, she supposed a spray of roses, could she get blood thorn too? Yes. He looked surprised but agreed she could do that and held out his hand to grasp hers firmly again. He'd leave now. He handed her his card, and she would contact him with the church details once she'd agreed them with the chaplain. And, oh yes, newspapers too, he called back as he approached the door. If she wanted the death notice to appear the next day, best move on that soon.

The chaplain's limp handshake suggested a belief in an afterlife – Grace had not died, merely passed on, and to that better place where pain and suffering were no more. Sadly, however, the funeral slots at Saint Mary's for Friday were already fully booked up, for an elderly parishioner at ten o'clock mass, and mass for the returned remains of an Irish-American at eleven. He could fit her in on Saturday though, or she might be buried from another church, but then what of the church choir with whom she'd always sung? Saturday, then. And he could, as of now, fit her in at ten or eleven, whichever was preferable. Ten? He nodded, then wrote it into his diary in a neat hand. And he'd liaise with the local clergy again and with the choir in relation to the ritual.

'We can lay her out together,' the attendant offered as he left too.

'I'll go buy a dress for her, for that.' Rose grasped the prospect as an excuse to escape and made for the door.

As she drove towards the local boutique she found life continued all around her in its amazingly normal way. Through green lights that still changed fast to orange, then to red, behind tardy buses as they edged their usual way along routes seven, eight and forty-six, as their ads offered futile assurances of pensions and life cover. The traffic slowed as it always did on the seafront and paused as usual at the zebra for a gaggle of schoolchildren to cross then pause and hop from square to square at the faded hopscotch map chalked on the pavement beyond. She slowed again behind a tourist bus, and her hand drummed impatiently on the wheel as tourists piled out, paused to click their cameras at the sea view, then made their way in a long line towards Joyce's tower. Then farther on still, to where the early summer chestnuts bloomed as always in white candles behind the hotel wall and close by the nearby boutique.

'You've heard of our end-of-season sale?' The shop girl was eager in the empty shop as she gestured towards a near rail.

'Not today.'

'They're all reduced. Half price. Some new arrivals already in. In summer colours,' she beamed, 'lilac.' She held a dress before her. 'This might suit you. What size? Twelve? Go on, spoil yourself, try it on.'

'It's for a gift,' she lied, and thought of Grace as she spoke, as if she still lived, in her favoured vibrant colours. And she shook her head.

'This, then?' A deeper shade this time, a mauve that veered into purple.

'No, I don't think so. Might I just look around?'

'Of course.'

She flicked from dress to dress, then from rack to rack.

'I can give you a gift voucher if you prefer,' the girl offered after a time.

'No, I'll find something.' She did, in the end. A simple dress that was cream-coloured and with a swirled skirt.

The tissue paper crinkled as the shop girl folded it softly. 'The colour will suit her?'

'Oh, I need matching shoes.' She looked around frantically, in the knowledge that she couldn't bury her friend bare-footed.

'We've a small selection. How about these?'

'You have them in size five?'

'Yes, and I've the perfect bag to match.'

'Just shoes, thank you.'

'We'll have more of our new summer selection in next week. You must call again soon.'

'Thank you.'

They dressed Grace's remains, put on her lace bra with its false breast first, then her panties with a matching slip, a pair of tights, and finally the new dress. Rose lifted the remains awkwardly as the attendant slipped the garment over her head then fitted her rigid feet, with difficulty, into the sandals. And her head? Would she have wanted the wig or no? Rose glanced to where it rested on the nearby locker, a fringed oval of shiny black nylon that fell straight as Grace's had, and placed it on her head. Severe against her now-pale face. She tried the scarf then, held it across her forehead, then discarded that too and left her lie, head bare. Then together they slid her from table to coffin and saw her nestle in the velvet lining, hands joined, as the attendant entwined her ringless fingers with a rosary beads. An open bible on a nearby table, its ribboned purple marker open at Isiah. *See I do not forsake you, I hold you in the palm of my hand.* A second mother of pearl rosary beside, and next to that a silver container and sprinkler that held holy water. Finally they placed four tall candles at each corner of the coffin and lit them one by one as Rose watched them flicker and cast their light and shade message across Grace's dead face; then a distinct smell of melted candle wax wafted towards her as it dripped its *Pax Christi* message.

Rose sat into the church pew beside Pete and looked around her. She watched the church fill through tired eyes – the pews close by Saint Anthony's shrine first, then those on the far side by Saint Jude's filled too – while before her and to her left the shrine of the Virgin reigned fresh with summer flowers. She averted her gaze from the coffin, tried to, yet was drawn to it, high on the main altar, red roses entwined with blood thorn atop.

To her left the choir shuffled, nervous she sensed, for the ritual they'd arranged and for one of their own. The distinctive smell of incense wafted towards her, then a shuffle of feet as all stood, followed by the *Kyrie* sung by their new soloist.

Rose left her pew, hands damp with nerves, the requested reading in her hand, then stood on the altar and faced the congregation. A sea of faces that looked towards her. She sought among their number to find Pete again, and felt better when their eyes locked and held. *The Lord is my Shepherd,* she stammered, *there is nothing I shall want.* The words dust on her tongue.

'Glad that's over?'

'Yes. Thanks.'

'You sounded fine.' He squeezed her hand.

Father liberal trendy had selected the parable of the talents for the gospel. Followed by the offertory prayers. She watched several mourners queue to read, one she recognised as a friend from the G&R, a colleague from work, a distant cousin who'd flown in from Edinburgh. They thanked many parties in turn: the hospital staff, her friends (Rose lowered her gaze at being included there), and all those who'd shared her love of music. New soloist again who sang the *Ave Maria*, Schubert' s when Grace had always favoured Gounod. Rose wished it were over, wondered, as she glanced around, if in time they'd find a manner to bury their dead in some other way. Didn't know and was too weary to care.

Inside the graveyard gate they followed the hearse on foot, beneath high yew trees and between rows and rows of tombstones. A number of huddled groups, among them several of Grace's old school friends, an arthritic Miss Behan with a walking stick; members of the church choir, with their new soloist who had sung so well now the centre of their attention; a group from Import-Export that had closed for the morning and put a notice in the newspapers to that effect; and a crowd from G&R, one of whom carried a large wreath from them.

Rose walked with Pete, out of character in his sombre suit and black tie, felt him squeeze her hand reassuringly as they approached the open grave. She glanced around the group that circled it and caught Brendan's eye, and he nodded towards her. The high mound of freshly dug earth stood damp with rain, and she watched the undertaker pile the floral tributes atop it. The fairest of May flowers, late daffodils, narcissi and crocuses, coupled with early summer roses, and an occasional rare orchid. In sprays, in bouquets, and some in wreaths. She searched among them for the roses and blood thorn she had sent, knew it was there somewhere, but couldn't find it. Noted how of the sympathy cards that were damp with soft rain, the ink had run on their messages, while others, cellophane covered, remained dry. The pale coffin was carried from the hearse and placed close to where the priest stood, and she heard him, as if from a far distance, read.

In the name of the resurrection ... Her gaze wandered to the coffin and she thought of the remains she knew were inside: Grace, eyes closed, limbs stiff, heart still, already disintegrating. She felt Pete's hand firm, warm against her shoulder. Prayers floated her way again. *Our Father, who art in Heaven*, and the murmured response. *Give us this day our daily bread.* Then *Hail Mary, full of Grace*, and the low-voiced reply from the group, *Holy Mary, Mother of God*, followed by a decade of the rosary.

The soft sound then of water sprinkled on the coffin, and the tiny droplets that settled on its brass plate that bore her name. She whimpered as it was lowered slowly down, down into the grave, heard the clump of earth thrown in after as it echoed dully from deep below. *Dust thou art, and unto dust thou shalt return.* Mourners queued around her to follow the earthen sod with single red roses. She saw the flowers descend down into the darkness, and followed them with a single red rose of her own. Green baize-covered planks then to cover the void with floral tributes placed atop. It was done.

The mourners began to dissipate. Rose saw Paul, who'd

stood at the edge of the crowd, walk quickly away. Others lingered to converse in quiet voices as a manager from Import-Export approached Pete. 'Bad business, this. A real loss to us. Knew the computer game from the start.'

'Old friend of Rose's here. You've met my wife?'

'Hi, I've heard Grace talk of you.' She heard their conversation progress to business matters, to Europe and the CAP, to the new export drive. Was Paul involved, and what were its chances of success.

'Rose?'

'Oh, hello.' She looked at the younger and unfamiliar female face blankly.

'I just thought "thank you for the music", all through. Didn't you?'

'You were ...?'

'Oh I just sang in the church choirs, and in the chorus at G&R, always wanted to sing as well as her. Ah, well.'

'We knew each other from way back, from school. Oh, hello, have you met Brendan, work colleague of mine?'

'Take care, Rose, you've had a bad fright and a rough week.'

'You'll say hello to Miss Behan, Rose.' A hand touched her arm. 'Long retired now, but she just insisted on attending.'

'Brave to the last, I believe,' their old teacher murmured. 'Quite a little heroine, wasn't she?'

The bedroom in Grace's apartment smelt of sick. Rose gagged at the pool of congealed vomit and the phone receiver that dangled loosely above it. She replaced it gingerly in its socket, hitting against the cassette player's start button in the process. It played eerily. Callas. *One Fine*

Day. She slammed the switch to silence and an open tube of mints spilled to the floor and mixed with the vomit there. Soapy water and disinfectant; she gagged again as she cleaned it, then opened the bedroom window wide and welcomed the fresh summer breeze against her face.

Get well cards everywhere, how she hated them now as they crowded the living room's mantel; she drew her arm across them and saw their rainbow symphony of lost hope fall to the floor. A hand-drawn card from Ann somewhere there, one too from Pete; she scooped them all up quickly into a large sack then left it stacked against the sofa.

The cancer aids, best clear them first, face the worst part and get it over with. Two crutches, unused, leave them in the hall for collection, beside the walking frame, unused too. Where were the wretched nylon wigs? There, on the wardrobe's top shelf, three in all, one in a short office style, the longer for hoped-for social wear, and the third, unusually long, as she'd waited for re-growth, as consolation. And several bright scarves she'd worn with her usual bravado. Hurled them all into the black sack atop the cards. Pulled out drawers then until she found the three bras, all of which boasted one fleshless breast each, into the sack too. And, worst of all, all those medicines that had failed; she lined the five small bottles atop the toilet cistern, prised off their plastic caps one by one then heard the pills drop with a small ping into the bowl below. The pills in pop packages took so much longer, to be prised free one by one; she sat on the toilet as she pushed them from their tinfoil bubbles. Sat there then for what seemed a long time after they'd flushed away.

But there was still work to be done, and best clear the perishables next. The fridge that still held food. Included an unopened carton of milk, a half-used tub of butter, an opened pack of rashers, how she'd grown to love bacon as one of the few foods she could taste. The freezer? It held half a dozen or more untouched dinners that Rose had so carefully selected for her, and she gritted her teeth as she piled them with the rest into a second plastic sack. The pantry with its dry stores, her favourite coffee beans, the pack half-used then carefully resealed, and loose tea, Barry's gold blend, only the best, of course. And, in a higher press, several cookbooks, a more recent cordon bleu with a page turned down at the corner at the recipe for pear and almond tart. The phone rang suddenly and so loud in the empty apartment that it made her jump.

'Pete. It's you.' Relief. 'Hi.'

'I'll come over if it'd help, offer still stands.' The tension drained from her but she shook her head. 'Stay with Ann, it's better that way. She's hardly seen us all week. No, I don't want her here, it's too bleak by a mile.'

'Drive in with her and meet you somewhere nearby for lunch?'

'No, honest, I've brought a sandwich. Thanks, but I'd prefer to stay with it, get it finished and done with.'

'Your choice. If you insist.' He sounded disappointed. 'Want to say hello to your daughter?'

'Sure. Hi, Ann. How's my love?'

'Dad said we were all going out for lunch.'

'Yes, Dad'll look after you. He might even buy you ice-cream too if you finish all your meal.'

'Alright.'

She heard the click at the far end as the phone changed hands again. 'Don't worry for her, she's fine. And you take care.'

'You too.' She returned the phone to its socket.

She cleared the bathroom quickly, the toothpaste tube that was half-used and carefully half-rolled to avoid wastage; strange how she'd never imagined Grace as economical in that way. Beside a newly opened bar of scented soap and a near-empty shower gel. All binned. Followed by dusty hair shampoo and conditioner, and the strange lotion she'd used to clean her wigs. And, surprisingly, behind the mirror door a toilet bag that held male shaving gear; she held it for a time, toyed with returning it to Paul then watched it follow the other discards into the large sack.

The living room took longer. She stood before her wall-to-wall shelving and realised that Grace had never once discarded a musical score. Sheet music to her left, her friend's handwriting occasionally neat in its margins. Programmes from the shows in which she'd taken such pride: *Oklahoma*, *West Side Story*, *The King and I*, all signed by the cast. She held the sack wide and piled them in, then opened a second plastic bag to fill with dusty 78s, saw Gilbert and Sullivan and *High Society* disappear deep within it, followed them with the newer eight-tracks: *The Sound of Music*, *South Pacific*, *My Fair Lady*, and finally the newest cassette, *Jesus Christ Superstar*. 'Charity', she wrote firmly on yet another label, then dragged both bags to the hall, one for the dump, the other for second-hand shoppers, and left them with the others already there.

Once the living room was clear she paused for lunch, poured the coffee she'd brought from its flash and drank it with the ham and cheese sandwich she'd made hastily earlier that morning. Switched on the TV news as she ate. Belfast again. Another bomb, in a pub this time, it had targeted football fans as they watched a match; bodies being hauled from the rubble, then the usual denunciations from cardinals, bishops, politicians on all sides, then a commentator who explained it all, it was in retaliation for— She switched it off dispirited and returned to her task.

The bedroom dressing table, still crammed with bottles and jars. She tore yet another plastic bag from the roll and piled them in. A bottle of cleanser first, almost empty, followed by a new one, still unopened. Then a half-full bottle of toner. Two brands of face creams, two jars, French brand and expensive, one for day and one for night. Foundation tubes, two as well, one for day and one for evening wear. Several lipsticks in the bright red and peach colours she favoured. A rouge brush, its bristles still dusty red with powder. Followed by a selection of eyeshadows, greens and browns, with two black mascaras, one for day and one for evening as well. Then hair tongs, hair rollers, a hair brush and two combs. A perfume spray, French again. Unopened cosmetics too, a perfume, unused, not her brand – had this been a gift? – and two further lipsticks, pink and a louder shade, almost purple. The black bag felt heavy as she lifted it and, fearful it would burst and spill its contents onto the carpet, she pushed it into a second heavy plastic sack then dragged it to the hallway too.

Her underwear and bedwear could be dumped as well, while the outer clothes might go to the charity shop. One wardrobe section held winter outfits, still cellophane wrapped from the dry cleaners, three office suits, an expensive wool coat and rain mac; she linked the hangers together then brought them to the hall too. An array of summer outfits in another section, all in the spicy yellow, orange and red shades she favoured. And shoes. What a vast array. Few flats, how many with a lower heel for daywear, and sandals with a high instep for social occasions.

The small drawer in the bedside chest was locked and she turned the key and opened it, guilty at what she might find inside. Tumbled its contents onto the empty bed beside her. Pearl earrings attached by gold clasps to cream velvet-coated cardboard, a sweat-stained red t-shirt. A card of Skellig Michael, its wild and primitive stone face lashed by Atlantic seas, 'It is done' written beneath it in an unfamiliar hand, and with that the stub of a boat ticket from Liverpool. An expensive necklet, the gold cold against the bare mattress, with a floral gift card signed in Brendan's familiar scrawl; a race card from a meeting at Leopardstown. She scooped them with her hand, held the black bag wide open, and watched them fall one by one inside it.

The second bedroom that Grace had used as a study was so much easier to tackle. She pulled two large cardboard boxes from the foot of the wardrobe and filled them, one with her business and work affairs, the other with her personal finances. Then phoned her solicitor's home number.

'The late Miss Donovan? Yes?' He paused, and she paused too, unsure of her reception on a Saturday.

'Rose Leahy,' she explained hurriedly, 'we were very old friends. I've just cleared her apartment.'

'Can't this wait 'til Monday?' he asked coolly.

She ignored his comment and spoke quickly, fearful he would put down the phone. 'I've stored all her legal and financial stuff,' she explained, 'it's in two large boxes, apartment deeds, share profile, bank statements, credit card details, you'll handle all that, I believe. Could one of your clerks collect them?'

'I suppose we could do that,' he agreed reluctantly.

'Saturday next?' she pressed hopefully.

'Ah, Miss Leahy,' he said, as if he'd suddenly remembered her from the funeral, 'of course. All my clerks work office hours, Monday to Friday I'm afraid.'

'Oh. Late Friday then.'

His voice grew amicable. 'You're the little one's mother?' he asked genially. 'Ann, I believe that's her name?'

'Yes, Grace was Ann's godmother.'

'Estate, sizable amount, all been bequeathed to her. Have the will here, will hold it in trust for her.'

She looked back from the hall door and surveyed her handiwork, the black plastic sacks piled up in the hallway; those labelled for the dump to the right and for the charity shop to the left, and the two cardboard boxes on the table for collection by her solicitor's clerk and her computer firm. Then she swore softly for the food bag had begun to leak; a small pool of water oozed beneath it, so she pulled it free from the others to take down to the garage and dump straight away. And, as they'd agreed, Pete would look after the rest. She walked from room to room for one last time, closed each door behind her one after another. All clear now save for the furnishings, and the charity shop would take those too. Place stripped bare of human presence and warmth. Soon the 'for auction' sign would go up, with 'executor's sale' blazed across it in red capitals and the promise of a bargain.

'Dead? What's "dead",' Ann asks.

Mam cries again and Dad holds her, then Mam goes up to bed and Dad tells Ann to take out her jigsaw so that they'll make a picture together. The picture is of a robin, but he's not bright and beautiful, he's horrid. She kicks the picture and breaks it all up again and cries too. Dad tells her to be quiet and not to wake Mam. She shouts that she will cry and runs to the stairs to go up to Mam but Dad stops her. Is Mam gone too, gone away, like Grace? She screams and kicks but he won't allow her upstairs to see, then tells her to get her book so and that they'll read a story together.

'Dead? What's "dead"?' she asks again.

Grace is lost somewhere and can't be found. Ever again. Like a sandal she left on a beach that was washed away by the ocean and never brought back. Gone. Forever and ever.

'How long is forever?'

'Grace is in heaven,' he says in his weary voice.

'Where's heaven?'

'Up in the sky. She's with God there.'

'But why did God take her?'

'He wanted an angel who could sing.'

'But when'll she be back?'

'I don't know.' He's tired too, like Mam, everyone's tired, and she is as well.

'I want to go to bed,' she says suddenly.

'Fine. Just have your milk and biscuit first.'

'And say night-night to Mam?'

'Not tonight.'

'But why?'

'Your Mam's exhausted,' he shouts, 'and so am I. Now don't be so goddam selfish, just this once.'

'What did I do? What did I do?'

'Have you homework? Get your copy and I'll help you. Copy the headline, write what's there.'

'No, I won't.'

'Ann, don't be impossible, we've all had a hellish week.'

'I'll write.'

'That's a good girl.'

'Dead. How d'you spell it?'

'Ann, no, you don't write that.'

'I will, I will.'

'Alright, if you must.'

'Look, I made a mess, but I don't care. Is Grace with all the lost things?'

'*You're* here, Ann.'

'Hmm.' She looks down to her feet and wriggles her toes, then kicks her legs, moves her arms and shakes her head. 'I can make a gingerbread man?' she asks suddenly in a brighter tone.

'Maybe tomorrow.'

'And sing? *All things bright and beautiful* ...' But she can't, for it makes her cry.

The Lord God makes them ... and then ... *like her new sandal that she lost on the beach and the sea washed away, never to return.*

'Grace was gone. Forever and ever. Not to return.' But she doesn't really believe that. 'How long,' she sobs again, 'is forever?'

A Year Later

When Rose visited Grace's grave she found the earthen mound fresh with young grass and whitened by frost that glittered in the dawn sun. She lay the spray of yellow and white roses close by the gravestone, then stretched out her hand and slowly traced her fingers across the name 'Grace Donovan' carved deep in black capitals. 'Aged thirty-seven', her hand traced that too, and finally letter by letter across the wish that she rest in peace. Close by, noises from the awakening city already beckoned as she began to hear the first sounds of morning life. A fog warning that hooted from the nearby pier while night fishermen unloaded their dawn catch beneath it. And close by, shop shutters rattled open and merchants threw clean water onto the pavements outside. Milk carts stopped and started in noisy delivery while the local bakery filled the air with the aroma of daily bread. Pedestrians rushed to queue at bus stops and train stations for their city-centre jobs. Car commuters piled up too, bumper to bumper, and already harassed mothers prepared their children for school.

'Goodbye, Grace. I still miss you.'

Rose left, walked beneath high yew trees and between the rows on rows of silent tombstones until she came at last to the cemetery gates. Once outside she crossed at the pedestrian light and made her way to her car. There she turned her ignition, adjusted her driving mirror and pulled out into the noisy traffic to join the living, and throw her lot in with them.